M000234581

CONTENTS

CORGI CASE FILES

CASE OF THE

DYSFUNCTIONAL
DAREDEVILS
BOOK 9

J.M. POOLE

Secret Staircase Books

Case of the Dysfunctional Daredevils

Corgi Case Files, Book 9

J.M. Poole
www.AuthorJMPoole.com

Sign up for Jeffrey's newsletter to get all the latest corgi news— Click here

A frappin' dog is a happy dog!

Case of the Dysfunctional Daredevils
Published by Secret Staircase Books, an imprint of
Columbine Publishing Group, LLC
PO Box 416, Angel Fire, NM 87710

Book layout and design by Secret Staircase Books
Cover images by Felipe de Barros, Yevgen Kachurin

* * *

Publisher's Cataloging-in-Publication Data

Poole, J.M.
Case of the Dysfunctional Daredevils / by J.M. Poole.
p. cm.
ISBN 978-1649140357 (paperback)
ISBN 978-1649140364 (e-book)

1. Zachary Anderson (Fictitious character)--Fiction. 2.
Pomme Valley, Oregon—Fiction. 3. Cozy mystery—Fiction. 4.
Corgi dogs—Fiction. 5. Amateur sleuth—Fiction. I. Title

Corgi Case Files mystery series : Book 9.
Poole, J.M., Corgi Case Files mysteries.

BISAC : FICTION / Mystery & Detective.

813/.54

ACKNOWLEDGMENTS

As always, this book's existence has only been made possible by a long list of people. First and foremost, my wife, Giliane. She puts up with me on a daily basis, she (politely) listens as I try to add some humor and jokes to the story, and then (mercilessly) shoots me down when something doesn't work with the story. For that, I'm eternally thankful, m' dear!

There are my Posse members, who have given me input on just about everything from suggesting fonts for the cover's typography, all the way down to lending a hand with character names. They take the time out of their busy schedules to render aid when I need it the most. Jason, Carol M, Caryl N., Diane, Mefe, Louise, and Elizabeth. Thanks, guys & gals, for everything you do for me.

Taking on the responsibility of creating the cover was, once again, Felipe de Barros. This Brazilian artist has proven himself time and time again. Thank you for all your hard work, amigo!

I also need to give a shoutout to my niece, Kaylee H. I asked her if she'd be willing to give me some help creating a few of the Daredevils, and she agreed. Thanks to her, we have the characters of Cecilia "Dagger" Jade and Caleb "Techie" Gyserman. I also asked for a description of their personalities, what they like, don't like, and even what they wear. To say that she delivered would be an understatement! Thanks for all your help, kiddo!

Finally, my thanks go out to you, the reader, for allowing me to continue the adventures of Zack and the dogs. I promise I'll try to keep up with Sherlock & Watson's ongoing exploits!

The graphic I'm using at the head of each chapter was found at: https://wikiclipart.com/mountain-clipart-black-and-white_34097/. Now, I don't know who is responsible for making it, but I do offer my thanks for making it available.

Now, without further ado, let's find out what's going on in Pomme Valley!

J.

For Giliane —

*There are no words which will adequately describe
how lucky I am to have you in my life. You mean
the world to me! Love you always & forever!*

B e careful," an exasperated voice said, for the third time in as many minutes. "There are jagged rocks everywhere. If you get hurt, then we're screwed. There isn't any help for miles, and I'm pretty sure neither of us have reception on our phones."

"If you're that concerned," a female voice shot back, "then you shouldn't have brought me all the way out to the middle of nowhere. I don't care how pretty the scenery might be. Nothing is worth this."

"I did mention this is a stratovolcano, didn't I? It's worth it, I assure you."

"I don't care if it's Mount Olympus. Look how steep that is. I'll never make it up there."

"The goal isn't to get to the top."

"It isn't? Then what's the point of doing all this?"

The first speaker, a man in his late twenties, gave an exasperated sigh. He took his companion's hand in his own and gave it a reassuring squeeze. Then he pointed northeast.

"There, at an elevation of over 7,000 feet, is a scenic point that overlooks Rascal River Valley. You can see for miles, in all directions. That, alone, is worth the trek up there. Don't worry. We're not going all the way to the top."

"How high is the top?" the woman, also in her late twenties, irritably asked.

"Over 9,000 feet. It's a doozy."

"You're a doozy," the girl quietly grumbled to herself.

"Do you know who this volcano was named after?" the man asked.

"Did they make a movie about it?"

"Er, no. Why would they?"

"Then no. Of course, I don't know who this blasted mound of rocks was named after."

Oblivious to his partner's sarcastic response, the man eagerly pressed on.

"John McLoughlin. He was a Chief Factor for Hudson Bay Company. This magnificent beast was so named in 1838."

"Great. Whoopee."

The man finally turned to his hiking companion and frowned.

"Listen, I know you don't care too much about this sort of thing, but it's important to me, okay? Could you at least try to look interested?"

"You're a geology major," the woman returned. "I get it. You like rocks."

"And you don't? I thought your profile said you enjoyed being outdoors."

"I do enjoy being outdoors," the woman angrily returned. "However, traipsing several miles over rugged terrain is not my idea of a good time."

"Okay, that's a fair point. I'm sorry."

"And I'm sorry I ever used that damn dating service," the woman muttered.

"Look over here," the man exclaimed. "Do you see this? This appears to be basaltic andesite. I do believe we're close!"

The woman sighed. "Thank goodness. My feet are killing me. I'd like to sit down for a while."

"Oh, I'm sorry. I meant the base of the volcano itself. The scenic point I was referring to is still about three hours away, so we'd better pick up the pace."

"I'd like to pick something up, all right."

"What was that? Do you see something you want to pick up?"

"No. I was just ... what's that?"

"What's what?"

"That. I'm talking about that right there. There's something poking out from underneath that bush by your left foot. Is that a piece of clothing?"

Noting a strip of bright yellow nylon near his left foot, the man bent to retrieve it, only he discovered it was entangled in the bush. The piece of fabric refused to budge, even after he had given the strip a good tug. Intrigued, the man gave the nylon strip a hearty yank, and then gasped with surprise as the object it was attached to came into sight:

the grisly remains of what was clearly a human hand. Strips of flesh could be seen dangling precariously from exposed, broken bones.

"That's it," the woman declared, catching sight of the mutilated remains. "No more computer dating for me. I'm outta here."

ONE

G lancing up at the sky, I nodded. It was gorgeous outside. The sky was a brilliant shade of azure, with white, puffy clouds visible as far as the eye could see. There was no wind, the temperature was holding at about 77 degrees, and thanks to the immediate drop in ambient temperature when the sun set, there was a feeling of fall in the air. All in all, it was my favorite time of year. Especially here, in southwestern Oregon.

Whereabouts in Oregon, you ask? Well, I may be biased when I say this, but I maintain this is the best part of the state. However, I do think the vast majority of the state is absolutely lovely this time of year, especially in the small town of Pomme Valley, which is where I currently live. Oh, I'm sorry. Let me introduce myself. My name is Zachary Anderson, but you can call me Zack. Everyone here does. I am in my mid-forties, I'm six feet tall, have brown hair (with what I keep telling myself is a gentle touch of gray) and blue eyes. I manage to keep myself in reasonable shape, and that's mainly due to me chasing after my two dogs.

Sherlock and Watson. Where to start with

those two? Well, they're both corgis. For those who are familiar with the breed, they will know there are two variants: those with tails (Cardigans) and those without (Pembrokes). My two are both Pembrokes. Sherlock, whom I've had the longest (but not by much) is tri-colored, and Watson is classified as red and white.

Go ahead and laugh at their names. Trust me, I've heard every joke imaginable. Sherlock was already named when I adopted him. As for Watson, well, I was told when I rescued her that ... yes, you heard that right. Watson is a she. She's a very sweet, timid little girl who loves to snuggle with her daddy and chew on her toys. As I was saying, Watson had been through a number of foster homes, too, and had been called several different names. However, when I accepted her into my home, she became Watson. Why? Well, lemme explain.

Sherlock and Watson, true to their namesakes, have a knack for solving mysteries, regardless of nature, be they murders, robberies, and so on. Somehow, and I still haven't figured out how, those two little dogs have the ability to locate clues pertinent to the case we're working on. Sherlock and Watson have solved more cases than the rest of the Pomme Valley police force, combined.

Oh. I should also mention that the three of us are official Pomme Valley police consultants. I'll get back to that in just a minute.

As I was saying, Sherlock and Watson have the

ability to sniff out clues that will, inevitably, link back to the case I'm working on in some fashion. Lately, I've gotten into the habit of taking pictures of anything that catches their interest, in the hopes of somehow being able to piece together what was happening first. But, has it helped? Not one bit. I can't begin to tell you how many times I've gone back through my pictures after a case has been solved and just shaken my head in disbelief.

Trust me, those two dogs are smart. Wicked smart. Smarter than me, even, only that's not saying much. So, yes, we're police consultants. Thankfully, those talents aren't called into service that often, so what do I do when we're not playing cops and robbers? Well, I'm glad you asked. First and foremost, I'm a writer. A romance writer, if you must know. Romance readers are a very dedicated lot and, once you've got them hooked on your books, they'll typically purchase anything that has your name on it. In this case, it isn't my name they're looking for, but my nom de plume: Chastity Wadsworth. Oh, I know that'll make a lot of you laugh. Then again, it also affords me a very decent living. Ever since moving here a few years ago, and rekindling my desire to write, my books have been burning up the charts.

And, if you don't think I stay busy enough with those two jobs, there's a third I need to tell you about. However, to be honest, it's not one that requires me to do much. I own a local winery, Lentari Cellars. It's a small, well, small-ish local winery that I inherited, which prompted me to move here in the first place. You see, I was married once before, to a lovely woman by the name of Samantha. Unfortunately, she was killed in an automobile accident a few years ago. To make matters worse, I found out last year that her death wasn't an accident. I won't go into details here, seeing how that's a story I've already told, but I will say I am thankful to put that painful experience behind me once and for all.

Now, here I am, engaged to ... look at that. I'm jumping ahead again. I really should introduce my fiancée, Jillian Cooper. She's five foot six, has auburn hair, and is in her late thirties. She's also the owner of a local business in town, Cookbook Nook. She and I hit it off right from the start, which pretty much startled the hell out of both of us. It probably has something to do with how many similarities the two of us share.

Let me give you a few examples.

First off, Jillian was a widow (lost her husband to cancer), and I was a widower. Then, we learned we both enjoy science fiction, be it movies, television, books, or magazines. And, we both love animals. Jillian loves dogs, only she hasn't had one for quite some time. Her late husband had been deathly allergic to animal dander, so she hadn't had the opportunity to be around that many. Well, Sherlock and Watson made sure that came to a screeching halt. Both of the corgis absolutely adore her. I think they love her just as much as I do, which brings me to my next point. I never would have thought love could strike me twice.

Thankfully, I was proven wrong. Jillian and I ended up getting engaged just a few months ago, while we were on vacation in Monterey. Even trying to take a simple vacation proved almost impossible, due to us discovering a dead body. It led to a strange series of events, involving a local numami ... nusimani ... coin collector, seeing how I have forgotten the technical term again, and the world-famous Monterey Bay Aquarium. During the wrap-up on that case, I gathered together our friends and family, unbeknownst to Jillian, and then popped the question, right there in front of everybody.

Like I said, that was several months ago. Now, summer was winding down and fall was rapidly approaching. The nights were cooling off, and before long, it'd be too cold to venture outside. Therefore, I have decided to see about having lunch with Jillian, outside at Casa de Joe's-- PV's best Mexican-food restaurant in town. However, my fiancée was currently preoccupied, teaching a cake-decorating class at her store. So, following her suggestion, I grudgingly decided to just have lunch by myself and perhaps work on my latest novel.

Snapping the leashes on both of the dogs, I grabbed my computer and headed out. The weather was warm, the sky was clear, and I decided to remove my Jeep's hardtop. Jillian didn't particularly care for riding in my Jeep in the open air. I guess it had something to do with getting windblown hair? I don't know. Speaking for us guys, as long as our hair is there, it can flap in the wind, turn gray, or turn bone white for all we care.

As for the dogs, this was the one and only time I've ever used seat belt restraints. After all, the last thing I need to worry about was to see one of the corgis stretched halfway over the side of the Jeep as they were enjoying the passing scenery. Trust me, it happened once. I vowed never to let that happen again.

Setting up my laptop before me on the open-air veranda at Casa de Joe's and then opening my work-in-progress to the current chapter I was on, I skimmed through the last two pages I had written to refresh my memory. However, try as I might, I just couldn't get the words to flow, and I wasn't sure why. I knew that writer's block was something every writer experienced from time to time. As for me, it had happened before, of course, but it was rare.

I found my mind jumping from topic to topic, like someone rapidly changing the channels on a TV set. When would the winery's new warehouse be completed? Would it pass all the necessary inspections? Could I really believe I was engaged to be married again? Would the weather cooperate on whatever date Jillian ended up choosing for the wedding?

On and on it went. I waited, fingers poised over

the keyboard, to see if my thoughts would settle down, but much to my dismay, they didn't. Sighing, I pushed back from my computer and reached for the basket of chips on the table.

Why couldn't I concentrate?

Movement in my peripheral vision attracted my attention. I glanced over to see what it was, and immediately cringed. It was a who and not a what. Willard Olson, postmaster of PV. He was also president of the Northwest Nippers herding dog club, and had been heckling me like crazy to get Sherlock and Watson to attend their monthly meetings. I had already been duped into allowing them to join, but I'll be damned if I give up any of my free time to spend it associating with that grump.

And that was why I was currently hiding behind a menu.

Once the walking beanpole had meandered by, I sighed in relief, and then noticed a group of teenage girls wandering this way. They had to be no more than thirteen or fourteen, which would typically have me recoiling with fright, only I recognized their ringleader: Zoe Woodson, daughter of Spencer Woodson. Zoe was a very bright girl, tall for her age, and had puppy-sat for me on several occasions. In fact, her eyes had just alighted on the two corgis and a wide grin appeared on her face.

"Oh, look! It's Sherlock and Watson! How are you two today, you adorable bundles of fur?"

Both of the dogs were wriggling with anticipation. Not only were they fond of Zoe, but they had spotted the gaggle of kids trailing behind. Before I knew it, both dogs had gone belly up and were receiving more attention than they knew what to do with. After a few moments of fervent scratches, Zoe looked up at me, as if she just now realized someone else was present.

"Mr. Anderson! Hello! I didn't see you there."

"Hi there, Zoe. Don't worry about it. I get that all the time. How are you and your friends doing today?"

"Just fine, Mr. Anderson. Are you here by yourself?"

I shrugged. "Just trying to get some writing done, only I can't seem to concentrate today."

Zoe nodded thoughtfully. "Well, you should take the dogs on a walk through the park. Throw the ball around. I know Sherlock and Watson both love that. It'll help you clear your head."

Zoe may only be thirteen, but she sure sounded a lot older. I smiled at the teenager and gave her a nod of thanks.

"I may end up doing just that. Shouldn't you be in school right now?"

Zoe grinned at me. "Parent-teacher conferences are happening today. We get the day off!"

"I remember those, and I won't even begin to tell you how many years ago that was. So, where are you off to?"

Zoe shrugged. "Anywhere other than home. We were thinking about catching a movie. There's a new CGI movie, with animated dogs in it, that looks really good."

I knew the movie Zoe was talking about, and it did not sound good in the slightest. Then again, to be fair, I was most certainly not in the movie studio's target demographics.

"I'm sure it'll be good. Have some popcorn for me. Good to see you, Zoe!"

"You, too, Mr. Anderson. And we will!"

I returned my attention to my laptop when a large family passed by. A large, loud family. I quickly glanced down at the dogs, to see how they were dealing with all the yelling, but thankfully, both corgis were content to watch. Realizing the fine art of people-watching was more entertaining than writing (for the time being), I closed my notebook and shut off my computer.

"Give that back to your brother, Timmy," the harassed young father snapped.

"But ... he's had his turn," a young boy of six or seven pouted. "It's my turn now!"

"Timothy Daniel," a woman's voice began, "if you don't give that electronic game back to your brother, then I'm confiscating it and you'll both be out of luck."

The seven-year-old slammed the game down onto the sidewalk in frustration. A wide-receiver who had just scored a tie-breaking touchdown couldn't have spiked the ball any better. The toy, understandably, shattered into a million pieces.

"That's it! I've had it! You've just lost all your

video game privileges," the father snapped. "All of you."

This brought cries of protest from the rest of the kids. I could still hear their screams of indignation well after I lost sight of them. I looked down at the dogs and ruffled their fur.

"Wow. Can't imagine what that household is like, can you?"

Another family then walked by. This one was the polar opposite of the first. The two kids, a boy and a girl who were probably five and six, were laughing, holding the hands of their parents, and clearly having a good time. The kids were well behaved, well mannered, and spoke when spoken to. Sherlock snorted once and then turned to look at me, as if he couldn't believe two families could be that different from one another.

"I know, right?"

"People watching, huh?"

The voice startled me more than I cared to admit, and I'm ashamed to say that I jumped in my chair, as though I had sat down on a buzzer. Even the dogs let out a few warning woofs. Then, both of them caught sight of who had spoken and they began wriggling with excitement. Again.

"Hey, Vance. How's it goin', amigo?"

"You're jumpy today. Where's Jillian?"

"Yeah, yeah. She's teaching a cake-decorating class and will be tied up for the next couple of hours. Since I have some time to kill, I thought I'd grab a bite to eat and work on my latest book."

Vance slid out a chair and promptly sat, which made me smile. He hadn't bothered asking for permission. Then again, he also knew he didn't need to, and that's what I liked about him.

"How's your day going?" I wanted to know.

"It's goin'," Vance admitted.

The waitress arrived just then and looked questioningly at my table's newest arrival.

"Good afternoon. Welcome to Casa de Joe's. Can I get you something to drink? A margarita, perhaps?"

Vance shook his head. "I'm still on duty. Do you have Dr. Pepper? I'll have one of those, thanks."

"You look stressed out, pal," I announced. "Overwhelmed at work? Is there anything the dogs and I can do?"

Vance shook his head. "No, I'm afraid not. I'm currently dealing with a rash of burglaries."

I perked up at this. "Oh? How serious?"

"Just some petty thefts. I suspect it's just a couple of bored teenagers. I've been trying to figure out how to catch them at it. Little punks."

Thirty minutes later, we were enjoying our lunch and watching a steady stream of people wander by. The waitress arrived with another beer for me, a refill for Vance's Dr. Pepper, and a fresh bowl of chips and salsa. I took a healthy pull from my bottle, grabbed a handful of chips, and leaned back in my chair. I had just caught my detective friend staring at me again, and if I didn't know better, I'd say he was working up the courage to ask me something. Curiosity piqued, I decided to wait for Vance to speak his mind. Whatever it was, I was pretty sure it wasn't police related, since if it was, he would have already said something by now. I know he's not a fan of my writing, seeing how he doesn't care for the romance genre, so it couldn't be that. The only thing left was the winery. What, did he want to put a hold on a bottle or two from the next batch of wine? Crossing my legs at the ankles, I stared at my friend and waited for him to tell me what was on his mind.

Vance caught me giving him a quizzical look and ended up chuckling. "Fine. You clearly know something is up. Well, you're right. I, uh, have a favor to ask of you. And, just to let you know, it's okay if you tell me no."

"What's on your mind?" I wanted to know.

"How long does it take for you to write a book?"

I blinked a few times. Of all the things that could have come out of Vance's mouth, this wasn't anywhere on the list.

"Huh? You want to know about my writing? Since when?"

My friend let out a nervous cough. "Er, please answer the question, would you? From start to finish, how long does it take?"

"From the time I think of an idea until a reader is holding a physical copy of the book?" I asked.

Vance nodded.

I grunted and gave the question some consideration.

"Well, when I first started writing, I was releasing one title a year. Now, I'm up to five or six. It usually takes me a month or two to write, depending how the story flows. Then, another month is spent on edits, rewrites, and formatting. All in all, about three months. Level with me, buddy. Where's this coming from? Why do you ask? Are you thinking about writing a book?"

"Hell no," Vance said, shuddering. "You gotta know your own strengths and weaknesses. Writing is definitely not a strength."

"Okay. Well, what's going on?"

"Look. Tori and I will be celebrating our 15th anniversary next summer. I wanted to do something for her that really stands out."

"And how do I fit into this picture?" I asked. "And congrats, by the way."

"Thanks. Listen, I was hoping I could get you to create a character in one of your stories based off of her. We both know she's a huge fan of your books. I'd like to see her face light up when she realizes she's reading about a character based on herself."

I pulled out a notebook and reached for my favorite mechanical pencil, which, as strange as it sounds, I always carry with me.

"So, do you want this story to be about her? Or, do you want the protagonist to look like her and have the same name?"

"Isn't that the same thing?" Vance asked.

I shook my head. "Not even close. I'll be honest, pal. I usually don't model characters off of people I know. But you and Tori are friends, and I will break my own rules for friends."

"I have no idea what to say to that," Vance admitted.

"You don't have to say anything," I told him. "Now, there's the easy way and the hard way. The easy way deals with me basing one of my protagonists off of Tori. I'll make her physically look like her, sound like her, adopt her mannerisms, vocal inflections, and so on. However, this character will still do what I want them to do and follow a specified plot."

"And that's the easy way?" Vance asked, incredulously.

"Yep."

"And, uh, what's the hard way?"

"That'd be uncharted waters for me," I answered. "I would listen to your ideas about a story, ask a lot of questions about what Tori likes and dislikes, and craft a fictional story around her."

"You've never done that before," Vance guessed.

I nodded. "Correct."

"Sorry, Zack. I never realized it'd be so much work. I'll just come up with something else to do for Tori. I don't want to put your other books on hold."

Vance finished off his soda and promptly

ordered a beer.

"Didn't you say you were on duty?" I casually asked.

Vance nodded and then glanced at his watch. "I was when I sat down, but now? I'm off. Forced time off, if you want to get technical. Chief Nelson said accumulating too much time off looks bad on the books, so starting next week, I'm on a forced vacation."

I grunted by way of acknowledgment. An idea had occurred, and I was busy jotting my notes while my memory was still fresh. Sadly, if inspiration struck, and I didn't write it down, then there wouldn't be a snowball's chance in hell I'd remember it at a future date.

"What are you writing in there?" Vance wanted to know.

"Ideas."

"Ideas? About what?"

"Ideas for a new period piece that just came to me."

"Would this have Tori in it?" Vance asked.

I nodded. "It would. Tori is Irish, isn't she?"

Vance nodded. "Right. Her mother's side of the family practically all came from County Cork, in Ireland."

"County Cork, Ireland," I softly muttered, as I hastily scribbled more notes. "That's perfect. Has she ever been there?"

"No," Vance said, shaking his head. "She's always wanted to go."

"Mm-hmm," I mumbled, as I added more notes.

"Just don't make her the bad guy," Vance pleaded.

Confused, I looked up. "Why would you say that?"

"You called her 'protagonist' earlier, didn't you? Isn't that the story's villain?"

"Pro," I clarified. "Protagonist is the hero, or heroine, for that matter. Antagonist would be your villain."

"Oh. Umm, are you really going to do this? Write a book about Tori?"

"I'm going to write a book set in the mid-19th century," I corrected.

"The mid-19th century?" Vance repeated, puzzled. "Why?"

"Hear me out, as this just came to me. From the years 1845 through about 1849, I believe, the Emerald Isle suffered through the great Irish Potato Famine. The vast majority of people either starved or died off. I'm thinking I'll set the story in County Cork, and have our story's heroine, Tori, battling unsurmountable odds as she struggles to keep her family alive during the worst catastrophe anyone has ever seen."

"Holy cow, she's gonna love that," Vance all but whispered, as a smile crept over his face. "She loves Irish stories, and anything pertaining to Ireland. Hey, umm, I may not know much about writing books, but, er, aren't you supposed to be writing stories your publisher wants you to write?"

I nodded. "Very true. Lucky for me, I have a completed backlog of five titles, which means if I wanted to take a year off, I could. As it happens, I'm not. Once I finish the title I'm working on now, I was planning on taking the next couple of months off. No, don't argue, pal. I can do this for you two. Consider it an anniversary present."

"But what if your publisher doesn't want to publish it?"

"Then I'll self-publish it," I answered. "Vance, don't worry. I've got this. This will be our secret. Well, I'll probably let Jillian know what I'm doing, but it'll only be the three of us."

"Can I pay you to do this?"

I shook my head. "Nope. As it is, if this book happens to take off, then, more than likely, I'll be splitting the proceeds with you guys."

"Do you need anything from me?"

I nodded, and pointed to Vance's jacket.

"It's time to pull out your notebook. I'm going to need to know anything you can tell me about Tori. Favorite color, favorite foods, where she likes to travel, likes and dislikes, favorite sayings, mannerisms, and so on. Do you see where I'm going with this?"

Vance was writing so fast in his notebook that I briefly thought the friction of lead on paper would light it on fire.

"I gotcha, pal. Thank you for this."

"It's my pleasure. I'll sketch out a possible out-line in the next couple of days, and when I do, we'll get together, go over it, and see if there's anything we need to change."

"I'm gonna owe you big, aren't I?" Vance groaned.

I grinned at my friend. "Oh, you'd better believe it, amigo."

"Have you and Jillian picked a date yet?"

"I think we have the date of our wedding narrowed down to fall, but that's it. September, maybe? I don't know. I just smile and nod whenever she asks me anything about it."

"September?" Vance repeated. "Wow. That's only a month away. You guys don't waste any time, do you?"

"Of next year, you nitwit," I chuckled. "We only got engaged earlier this year in Monterey, remember?"

Vance nodded. "Oh, right. Gotcha. Thought that was kinda quick."

"I'm thinking indoor wedding, but I know Jillian would love for the ceremony to happen outside. The problem with that is ..."

Vance looked up at me after I trailed off.

"What? What's the problem?"

At that exact moment, both corgis woke from their nap, lifted their heads, and looked out at the street. For the record, they noticed the same thing I had, which caused me to lose my train of thought.

I should explain. For the past fifteen minutes, Vance and I had been watching the people meander by on Main Street. For the most part, the townsfolk appeared happy, content, and intent on reaching their destinations without lingering too long in one spot. That's why he stood out so much.

I had trailed off the moment I clapped eyes on the guy. He was short, being no taller than five foot four. He had a slim, athletic build, dark brown hair, and a full, trimmed beard. If I had to guess his age, I'd say he was in his late twenties. I can't speak for Vance, but my eyes were drawn to this guy because of his outfit: faded blue jeans and a button-down, collared, maroon shirt. But the kicker was the floor-length black duster he was wearing. He almost looked like a young Chuck Norris, only thanks to that black jacket he was wearing, I could now picture him dodging bullets in slow-mo.

Proof positive I've watched too many movies.

I looked over at Vance, hooked my thumb at the strange sight, and indicated my detective friend should take a look. Once he did, Vance turned back to me with a quizzical look on his face.

"He sure sticks out, doesn't he?" he eventually decided. "I wonder who he is."

"Whoever he is, he's certainly not from around here," I added.

As if to prove my point, the stranger looked pointedly up at the nearest street sign, then stepped back a few steps so he could observe the passing townsfolk, and finally, pulled out his cell phone, as if to confirm an address. We saw the stranger look back up at the street sign, nod once, and then began to study the nearby businesses. He was clearly looking for something. After a few moments, he slid his phone back into an interior jacket pocket, but not before allowing us to see the butt of a gun sticking out of a shoulder holster.

"Did you see that?" I asked, as I turned to Vance.

My friend solemnly nodded. "Yeah, I did."

"Maybe he's a cop?" I suggested.

Vance shrugged. "Based on his outfit, he more than likely has a CCW permit. Ten bucks says he's looking for Wired Café."

I wordlessly pulled out a ten and dropped it on the table. Together, we watched the guy study the stores. Then, as if he knew we were talking about him, the strange guy suddenly turned and looked straight at us. The Matrix wannabe checked his phone again, nodded, and then started walking in our direction. Confused, I turned to Vance.

"I know he's not coming over here for me. What about you? Do you know him?"

"I've never seen him before," Vance assured me.

"Afternoon," the young guy said, as he arrived at the Casa de Joe's terrace. Damned if he didn't have a southern accent, too. Completing the picture was a subtle tip of his hat. "Would one of you be Detective Vance Samuelson?"

I turned to look at Vance, grinned victoriously, and snatched the money off the table.

"Told you he wasn't here for me. That's him, pal," I said, as I looked up at the stranger.

"I'm Detective Samuelson," Vance formally said, rising to his feet. "Can I help you with something?"

The bearded man nodded. "I hope so. I was told I could find you here. Ashley Binson, of the U.S. Marshal Service."

My eyebrows shot up. Did he just say his name was Ashley Binson? Wasn't that the name of an actress? I know I've heard it somewhere. And Ashley? You don't hear of many guys being called by that name. This one was a U.S. Marshal? And he's here, in Pomme Valley? Well, at least that would explain the getup. And the gun.

Vance automatically shook the guy's hand.

"Nice to meet you, Ashley."

"Call me Ash," the stranger insisted. Then, dropping his voice so that we could barely hear it, added, "And it sounds better."

Vance grinned. "Will do. So, what can I do for you, Mr. Binson?" Vance politely inquired. "We don't get many marshals around here. You're looking for someone, aren't you?"

Marshal Binson nodded. "I am. Is there somewhere we could talk? Privately?"

"This is Zack Anderson," Vance coolly replied, as he turned to give me a brief look. "He's one of the PVPD's police consultants. What you have to say to me can be said to him, too."

"As you wish, Detective."

"And you can call me Vance," my friend told the marshal. "Everyone does. Pull up a seat. Tell us why you're here."

"I'd like to know who told him you would be here," I quietly muttered.

Vance grinned as he looked across the table at me.

"I told Julie that I was going to see about tracking you down. You're not a hard person to find, Zack. And, if Mr. Binson here happened to stop by the station, then he would have found Julie manning the Help Desk. She knows your routine just as well as I do."

"Hardy har har," I grumbled, as I mentally vowed to change up my routine.

Marshal Binson noticed Sherlock and Watson, who were currently lying by my feet and had both locked eyes with him, and he drew up short.

"They let dogs into restaurants around here?"

I waved my arm around, indicating the current surroundings.

"We're not inside the restaurant, are we?" I pointed out. "As such, the animals are allowed up on the terrace, provided they don't go inside."

Marshal Binson shrugged and squatted down next to the dogs, "Suit yourself. Hey there, sport. Do either of you mind if I sit here?"

Sherlock sniffed the proffered hand once, snorted, and then returned his attention to the passing people out on the street. Watson gave the hand a single lick before she, too, turned back to watch the people passing nearby. Nodding appreciatively, Ash pulled out the chair next to Vance and carefully sat, as though he was in pain.

"You okay there, pal?" I asked, hesitantly.

"Yeah, thanks. It's been a long day."

"It's not quite one p.m. yet," I pointed out.

Ash shrugged. "True. However, I am stationed at the Western District of Texas. I drove straight here from my office. I guess you could say that I was tired of sittin' on my ass. Done enough of it in the last two days."

"You drove all the way here from Texas?" I repeated, amazed. "That's a long drive."

"You have no idea," Ash muttered. The marshal looked over at Vance. "You probably want to know why I'm here, don't you?"

Vance nodded. "The thought had crossed my mind. You specifically came looking for me, which means you checked in with my boss, who probably told you to check with Julie, who then told you how to find me. How am I doing so far?"

Ash shrugged. "Not bad. You come highly recommended. You don't disappoint. I'm hoping you can help me."

"Help you how?" I asked. "Are you working on a case?"

"He's looking for someone," Vance answered, before the marshal could respond. "U.S. Marshals are essentially the enforcement arm of the federal courts. They serve warrants, capture fugitives, and transport prisoners."

"That's an accurate, textbook answer," Ash idly commented. He reached for the glass of water the waitress had just set down and drank nearly half of it. "We also oversee the witness relocation program."

"Was Vance right?" I asked. "Are you looking for someone?"

Ash nodded. "He is, and I am. Your Chief Nelson has assigned Detective Samuelson to me, with the hopes of being able to help me out. Since he knows you didn't want to take a vacation in the first place, he figured that you should be okay working the case with me. And, if you're a police consultant, Mr. Anderson, then maybe you can help me out, too."

I immediately pointed down at the dogs.

"If you're looking for something, or in this case, someone, then we'll definitely need to get these two involved."

"I'm not currently tracking him," Ash pointed out, as he briefly glanced at Sherlock and Watson. "And besides, I'm sure bloodhounds would do a better job tracking a fugitive than cute fluffballs like these."

"You'd think so," Vance said, grinning, "but you'd be wrong. They've solved more cases in the last couple of years than anyone on the force."

"That's not something I'd openly admit," Ash chuckled.

"Oh, trust me, I usually don't," Vance acknowledged. "However, in this case, I also trust their instincts. So, you're in town, looking for someone. Who?"

Ash reached inside his jacket and pulled out a folded set of papers. He smoothed them out on the table before he began to read.

"Jerod Jones, age twenty-three. He's five-six, weighs 140 lbs., has brown hair, brown eyes, and a slim build."

"What's he done?" I asked.

"Held up a bank," Ash stated, his tone turning flat. "It went bad. Three hostages were killed. This happened in Texas, by the way."

"I figured," Vance commented. "Go on."

Ash flipped the page. "Jerod was sentenced to life in prison, only he escaped during a work detail. Murdered a fellow prisoner."

"Sounds like a model citizen," Vance quipped.

"How in the world did a mass murderer manage to escape?" I angrily demanded.

"By killing another inmate," Vance reminded me. "The specifics aren't what's important right now. Catching this guy is, however."

"How do you know he's in Oregon?" I wanted to know.

Ash shrugged. "He was last spotted in Portland. Apparently, he held up a convenience store. We figure he wanted some snacks, and then couldn't resist the temptation of picking up some extra cash.

Shocked, I held up a hand. "You're telling us there's a mass murderer loose? In Pomme Valley?"

Ash shook his head. "What I'm saying is that there's a chance Jerod is here in Pomme Valley."

"So, we'll keep our eyes and ears open," Vance promised. "I assume you have a picture of this guy?"

Marshal Binson slid his sheaf of papers over. Stapled to the front page was a 5"x7" photo of a young kid. Clearly, it was Jerod's mug shot, as he was seen holding up a small sign stamped with his case number. Vance and I leaned over the table and studied the picture.

This kid may have been twenty-three, but he looked sixteen. He had freckles on both cheeks, dark brown hair, and matching eyes. Jerod looked like he could be one of my neighbor's kids. He looked bright, cheery, and completely harmless. In fact, in my honest opinion, he looked confused, like he wasn't sure why he was having his photograph taken.

"That's our guy?" Vance incredulously asked, as he looked up at the marshal. "Doesn't look too dangerous, does he?"

"Don't let his looks fool you," Ash warned. "Jerod is a cold-blooded killer. Shows no remorse for any of his actions. Remember that convenience store in Portland? Well, Jerod shot and killed the owner of that Square L. Why? We don't really know. Security footage shows Jerod gunning down the owner in cold blood."

"Perhaps they didn't have the right kind of snacks?" I joked.

Marshal Binson turned to regard me as though he was just now realizing I was there.

"As crazy as that sounds," Ash admitted, "it could very well be the truth. However, I don't think we'll ever know."

"Awwooooo!" Sherlock suddenly howled, only it wasn't his normal howl but a low, guttural dad-you-need-to-see-this type of noise.

I looked up in time to see an older guy walking by on the sidewalk on the other side of the restaurant's terrace. He was wearing a bright red baseball cap, a black t-shirt, and camouflage pants. Noticing the guy was holding several boxes under each arm, and he was angling for a store which specialized in shipping services, I turned back to the dogs.

"What was that for? Stop it. They're just boxes, and he's planning on shipping them. Zip it, okay?"

Sherlock whined and looked over at Watson, as though he expected her to join him. Then, damned if she didn't do just that. They both looked at me and whined.

"Fine. Here, is this what you want?"

I reached for my phone, activated the camera app, and then—left-handed—snapped some pictures in the general direction the guy had gone.

Confused, Ash turned to Vance with a quizzical look on his face.

"It's a long story," Vance admitted. "The dogs are smart. If they see something, then it's worth noting. Zack takes the pictures, and somehow, the dogs know this, so they're satisfied."

"That makes absolutely no sense at all," Ash

said, as he eyed the dogs.

"It doesn't have to," I added, as I slipped my phone back into my pocket. "Now, as you were saying?"

"What was I saying?" Ash asked, as he frowned.

"Portland cops," Vance answered.

The marshal nodded. "Right, we were talking about Jerod's hold-up at the Square L."

"I'm surprised the Portland cops didn't get him," Vance said, shaking his head. "Those guys are some of the best. They usually have incredibly quick response times."

Ash nodded. "You're right. They do. Jerod was still there when they arrived."

Surprised, Vance and I shared a look.

"How'd he get away?" my detective friend finally asked. "Tell me he didn't kill someone else."

"He didn't," Ash confirmed. "What he did do, however, was disappear right from under their noses."

"How?" I demanded.

Ash shook his head. "Unknown."

"Do you have a theory?" Vance asked the marshal.

Ash grunted once. "I do. I think our perp is a master of disguise. I think he somehow managed to change his appearance and slip out with the rest of the bystanders."

"That's an awfully narrow window of opportunity," I pointed out. "Is that even possible?"

"It's just a theory that happens to fit the facts," Ash acknowledged.

"And this guy is now rumored to be in town," I grumped. "That's just spectacular. Vance, do you think the chief will appeal to the public to try and find this guy?"

"That'd more than likely incite unneeded panic," Vance answered, as he shook his head.

I glanced down at the dogs as a thought occurred. Neither one of them had been acting peculiar lately. If this Jerod person was in town, then wouldn't either of the dogs have noticed?

"When do you think he could show up?" I asked.

Ash sighed and sat back in his chair.

"All right, I'll admit it. He's already here."

"What?" Vance snapped. "He's already here? You have proof?"

"We followed Jerod here just over two months ago," Ash confirmed. "We learned that Jerod's former roommate was living here, so we set up a stakeout. It took nearly three weeks, but Jerod was finally spotted, but only briefly."

"And you're sure it was him?" Vance asked. His notebook was out, his head was down, and he was taking notes like crazy.

"I wasn't part of that stakeout," Ash confided. "Wish I was, though. That sumbitch would never have made it by me. I don't care what he was wearin'. Anyway, a buddy of mine was the one who spotted him, only there's nothing to back him up.

No pics, no video, no nothing."

"Why would you think he's still here?" I asked, confused. "This Jerod person sounds like a smart guy. He must've known he was being watched. Why stick around?"

In answer to my question, Ash reached inside his jacket and retrieved a crumpled, tri-folded piece of paper. From the looks of it, I'd say it was one of those pamphlets one would expect to find at a tourist center.

"What is that?" I wanted to know, as I slid the folded pamphlet over for a closer look. I looked at what was being advertised and then glanced up at our new friend. "You're kidding."

"It's proof he's here," Ash smugly informed us.

TWO

T hree days passed. It was now Friday night, and per our usual custom, our group of friends had gathered at a local restaurant for our weekly get together. We all took turns picking the restaurant-of-choice, and this time around, it was Julie's turn. Well, her favorite was a pizza joint by the name of Sarah's Pizza Parlor. I tried it for the first time when Jillian had gathered us all together to investigate her alleged ghost-infested investment house earlier this year. Sarah's had fantastic pizza, so there weren't any complaints coming from my direction.

"Do you see what this says? I'm talking about this little white square right here, man. It says that you must sign a Release of Liability form before your application will be considered. Umm, can we all say *hell no*?"

I grinned at my friend and reached for my beer. Hmm, I guess I should introduce the occupants seated around our large table. There's myself, my fiancée, Jillian; Vance and his wife, Tori; and Harry and his aforementioned wife, Julie. The six of us were laughing, cracking jokes, and were essentially having a great time. That is, we *were*. Vance took care of that when he *accidentally* brought up the subject of our meeting with Marshal Ash Binson earlier in the week, and his evidence that a mass murderer was hiding somewhere in PV.

The brochure Ash had produced turned out to be an advertisement for a group of thrill seekers, calling themselves the Dysfunctional Daredevils. Vance had inquired about the 'dysfunctional' part of the name. As for me, well, I zeroed in on the 'daredevils' side of it. Thrill seekers? I considered it a thrill if I got down to play with Sherlock and Watson on the floor, and my joints didn't sound like someone cracking their knuckles when I got back up.

"As I mentioned earlier," Marshal Binson had said, "Jerod is an adrenaline junkie. It's my belief that he's here in Pomme Valley, hiding in plain sight."

"As a member of this group?" Vance asked skeptically.

Ash nodded. "Yep. That's my theory."

"Does anyone else share your theory?" I wanted to know.

Ash sadly shook his head. "Afraid not. That's why I'm here. Alone."

"No backup," Vance guessed.

"No backup," Ash confirmed.

Fast forwarding to three days later, Vance let the cheaply printed paper casually drop out of his pocket while we were at dinner. Sitting closest to him was Harry, who snatched up the flyer the moment he spotted it. Unsurprisingly, his reaction had rivaled our own.

Harrison "Harry" Watt, town veterinarian and my best friend from high school, skeptically looked at each of us in turn. After a few moments, he polished off his beer and plunked it noisily back on the table.

"All I'm gonna say is that something like this is not for me. You two surprise the hell outta me. I never would've pegged either of you as thrill seekers. Especially you, bro," Harry said, as he turned to look at me.

Both Vance and I held up our hands in the universal time-out gesture at the exact same time. Neither of us noticed what the other did, in case you were wondering.

"I see that further clarification is required," I intoned, adopting a formal British accent. "Vance and I are in no way, shape, or form endorsing the idea that any of us join this ridiculous club. Speaking for myself, of course, I do believe I will say … pull your thumbs out of your ears, my good man. That is not what we said."

"Far from it, buddy," Vance agreed, sniggering loudly.

"I thought you said this guy is here because of this daredevil club," Harry protested.

"Who?" I asked. "That marshal dude or the guy he's chasing?"

"The guy he's chasing," Harry answered.

"Neither of us said anything of the sort," Vance contradicted. Catching sight of the person just now entering the pizza parlor's front door, my detective friend rose to his feet. He waved the newcomer over. "In fact, we can let him explain it. Marshal Binson, come on over. Let me make the intros. Zack you know. Sitting on his left is Jillian, his fiancée."

Jillian rose to her feet, prompting everyone to do the same.

"It's nice to meet you, Marshal. Zachary has told us a lot about you."

Ash had taken off his black cowboy hat the moment he walked through the door. He hung it and his jacket on a nearby peg and then shook Jillian's hand. He glanced over at me and nodded.

"Knowing how I am with first impressions, he probably told you I was a certifiable nutjob."

"Well, not in those exact terms," I said, grinning.

"On Jillian's left is my wife, Tori. Then, across the table, we have Harry and Julie Watt."

"Pleased to make y'all's acquaintance," Ash announced. "I appreciate the invitation. So, Zack, no dogs tonight?"

I gestured at the surrounding environment. "We're inside. No dogs inside. If this place had a terrace, then we'd be out on it and yes, the dogs would be there."

"I don't think I've ever met any corgis before your two," Ash said, as he slid in next to Harry.

"They're wickedly smart," I said. "Way too smart for their own good."

"Have they barked at anything else?" Ash wanted to know.

"How do you know they bark at certain things?" Julie wanted to know.

"They took an interest in some guy a few days ago," Ash explained. "Did that ever pan out?"

I shrugged. "Not yet, it hasn't. To answer your question, as a matter of fact, they did. Well, Sherlock did. Watson joined in a few seconds later."

"What'd he bark at?" Vance asked, interested.

"The grocery store."

"Gary's Grocery? Why?"

"I wish I knew."

"When was this?" Vance wanted to know.

"Earlier today," I answered.

"Did you take any pictures?" Jillian asked.

"A few. At least, I think I did. I was driving at the time, and am not sure I hit the camera shortcut properly. If I did, then there'd be a few shots in there. Then there was the gas station two days ago."

Vance's notebook put in an appearance. "Rupert's?"

"Yep. Not sure why. I was driving there, too, so I made the attempt to take a few pictures."

Ash nodded. "You lead an interesting life, Zack. So, you two, have you thought about my offer?"

"What offer?" Jillian asked, as she turned to me.

"Offer?" Tori repeated, at the same time.

"To join the daredevil club. They said they both needed to talk to y'all about it."

Our table fell deathly quiet. And, if possible, I heard the smirk form on Harry's face. A soft hand was placed over mine. Moments later, I felt her nails dig in.

"Zachary? Is there something you need to tell us?"

"For the record," I falteringly began, "we did not tell him we'd join this club. I will admit that, at the time, I had considered it. However, the more I think about it, the more I'm leaning towards 'no'. It's way too dangerous. I should have told you this last night, Marshal. Sorry, pal."

Surprisingly, Marshal Binson nodded, as though he had just heard pleasing news. He didn't say anything as he looked over at Vance. My detective friend had dropped his gaze to his beer and refused to look up.

"I'm in the same boat," Vance admitted. "Joining this club is not something people our age do. It's what someone your age does."

"I don't understand," Jillian suddenly said. "If you think this fugitive is hiding among the members of the Dysfunctional Daredevils, why not just stake out the clubhouse, so to speak, and arrest him when he shows up? I mean, it's not like you don't know what he looks like, right?"

Ash nodded. "That's true. The fault with that logic, I'm sorry to say, lies with one of Jerod's hidden talents."

"And that is?" Tori curiously asked.

"I personally believe he's a quick-changer."

"A quick-changer?" Harry repeated. His eyebrows shot up. "Wait. Are you saying you think he can change his appearance on the fly?"

Ash shrugged. "I personally think it's how he eluded capture before. To answer your question, ma'am, just because we have a picture of him doesn't mean it'll make it that much easier to find him."

"You think he's changed his appearance again," Jillian guessed.

Ash nodded. "That's correct, ma'am. The only way to know for certain Jerod is a member of this thrill-seeker club is for someone to sign up and get to know the members."

"This is a small town," Vance stated. "Everyone knows I'm a cop. If I suddenly show up and announce I want to join, and if Jerod is there, then that would undoubtedly scare him away."

"Actually, that's why you two are perfect," Ash argued. "How old are you guys? Late forties?"

"Kiss my ass, pal," Vance grumbled. "My fortieth is this year."

I guiltily raised a hand. "I'm sorry to say I've already celebrated my fortieth."

"Over ten years ago," Harry snickered.

I glared at my friend as the table erupted in laughter.

"Oh, yeah? You and I are the same age, amigo. That means you're as old as a dino doo, too, you know."

"But you're still older." Harry chuckled.

"Not by much," Julie announced, giving me a wink.

"As old as dino doo," Ash repeated, laughing. "I'm stealing that to use on a buddy of mine, who works in an FBI field office near my own. But, don't you see? If Jerod sees you guys in the club, then he'll assume you're suffering from some mid-life crisis and it won't come as a surprise to anyone."

"But I'm not suffering from any mid-life crisis," Vance protested. "I'm perfectly happy turning forty this year."

Just then, someone started wheezing. Short, rapid coughs came next. Vance's eyes narrowed as he turned to his wife.

"You okay there, Tor? Got a frog in your throat?"

"Did I hear that right?" Tori gasped, between breaths. "You? You're okay with turning forty? What alternate universe have we all somehow stumbled into?"

Vance frowned. "You think I have a problem hitting the big 4-0?"

"I know you have, dear. You're moody, irritable, and an all-around ..."

"... pain in the neck?" Harry helpfully added, after Tori trailed off.

"Some people don't handle getting old as gracefully as others," I stated.

It was Jillian's turn to snort. Tight-lipped, I

turned to her and crossed my arms over my chest. However, I couldn't hide the smile that had formed on my face.

"Got something to add, m' dear? Do you disagree?"

Jillian nervously cleared her throat before she finally turned to look at me. I could see that she was fighting back an extreme case of the giggles.

"Well, it's just that I've heard you complain about how much gray hair you have. I know you like getting older just as much as Vance does."

I automatically scratched the side of my head. "I don't have that much gray, thank you very much."

"I wasn't referring to your head," Jillian squeezed out, between giggles.

"Whoa!" Harry exclaimed, as he threw his hands up in a time-out gesture. "That's some serious TMI right there!"

"Eww," Vance frowned.

"Good grief," I scowled. "It's not what you think. Get your damn minds out of the gutter."

"Chest hairs," Jillian helpfully added. "Zachary has been complaining about gray chest hairs."

"Sure, you have," Vance snickered.

Tori fixed her husband with a stare.

"Do you really want to go there?"

"Do we have to talk about this here?" Vance hissed.

"I'm not trying to start an argument," Tori soothed. "Look. I think we might have been presented with an opportunity. I think Marshal Binson might be able to help you out."

"How?" Vance suspiciously asked.

"By joining this adventure group," Tori said. "Perhaps a touch of danger just might snap you out of your foul mood."

"You want me to risk my *life*?" Vance asked. "Am I hearing that right? I'm already a cop. Isn't that considered dangerous enough for you?"

"She's giving you the opportunity to go have fun, bro," Harry cut in. "Don't argue with her."

Vance looked over at me. "What about you?"

Caught with my bottle up in the air, I nearly choked as I found myself the center of attention.

"What are you dragging me into this for?" I demanded. "I've already had my fortieth birthday."

"Either I find someone to do this with me," Vance began, "or I don't go. I won't be that sad, pathetic loser trying valiantly to hold on to his youth."

"Are you really considering doing this?" I asked. "You're going to join the Daredevils?"

"Only if you will, too."

I confidently looked at Jillian, expecting her to be frowning and shaking her head. However, my fiancée's expression was far from disapproving. In fact, Jillian still looked as though she was trying to hold back a laugh. There was no way she'd be up for this, was there?

"You can't be serious," I began, as I looked at the beautiful woman sitting beside me.

"Do you really think they'd put you in harm's way?" Julie added, from across the table.

"I'm not really concerned about that," I explained, as I looked over at Harry's wife. "What has my attention is the simple fact that a mass murderer may be hiding within that group."

"I'm sure the marshal can guarantee your safety," Tori added, as we all looked over at our new friend.

"I wouldn't ask you to do this if I didn't think I could handle the situation," Ash informed us. "All you would be doing is observing. If you see something, then you two will not be doing anything about it. You'll contact me and I'll deal with it."

"But Vance is a cop," I protested. "I'm pretty sure that if he spots your fugitive, he'll probably be busy slapping handcuffs on the guy."

"True story," Vance agreed.

"I have a question," Jillian announced, and then promptly fell silent as she waited for everyone to quiet down. "If this Jerod individual is a master of disguise, how will Zachary and Vance know who to look for? Didn't you already mention that he probably doesn't look like his picture anymore?"

"She brings up a good point," I said, as I turned back to Ash. "I mean, what else can you tell us about him? Is there anything that would be helpful in picking him out of a lineup?"

Ash shook his head. "Jerod was a loner. He didn't have friends, and as far as I'm aware, none of his family have had any word from him in years."

"Then, who has?" Harry asked.

Ash shrugged helplessly. Right about then, I snapped my fingers. Hadn't the marshal indicated there was a reason why Jerod had chosen PV?

"What is it?" Vance wanted to know.

"Who does Jerod know in town?" I asked. "Why did he pick our city?"

"His former roommate," Ash reported.

"That's right," Vance said, nodding. "I had forgotten about him. Nice going, Zack. All right, Marshal, what say you and I go over and interview this roommate? He might have some insight into … what's wrong? Why are you shaking your head, Tori?"

"You're supposed to be on vacation," his wife complained. "For the next two weeks. Longer, if I had any say about it. But, I don't, and now you're committed."

"I'll owe you big," Vance admitted. "Start thinking what I can do to make this up to you, and I'll do it."

That earned my detective friend a few hoots and hollers from our table.

"What are you going to have to do?" Tori wanted to know.

"We have to keep an eye out for this Jerod individual. Zack and I could watch the club, and Ash here can watch the roommate."

"That won't be possible," Ash solemnly answered. "The roommate is dead. He was killed in what officials are calling an accident."

"What kind of accident?" Julie wanted to know.

"I'm not gonna like the answer, am I?" I muttered.

Overhearing, Jillian gave my hand a reassuring pat.

"We're assuming it's a skydiving accident," Ash answered.

"Skydiving," I grumbled. "Swell. Wait. Are you insinuating the Daredevils are somehow involved? Was the death ruled accidental?"

"I don't know if you've ever examined a body that's fallen from the sky," Ash slowly began, "but, um, there really isn't much a medical examiner can, er, determine."

The color drained out of my face as I realized what the marshal was suggesting. All three ladies paled and looked away. Both Vance and I shuddered and fidgeted uncomfortably in our chairs. Our table fell silent, as the five of us—not counting Ash—knew it would be considered bad form to discuss severely mangled human remains while at dinner.

Did you notice I said *five*? The table's sixth occupant, unfortunately, wasn't known for his morals or his common sense. Apparently, Harry wasn't born with a censor between his mouth and his brain, either.

"Hah! Dude, that guy would've been nothing more than a hamburger patty. Any medical examinations would have been impossible, man. Every single bone in his body would not only be broken, but smashed into a million pieces. Wouldn't that be a sight to see?"

"Harrison!" Julie hissed. "We all know what it means. Seriously? We're eating pizza, for crying out loud."

Harry shrugged. "Oh. Too much?"

"Are you really a veterinarian?" Ash asked, amazed.

"He doesn't sound like it, does he?" I joked, as I gave my old high school friend a grin. "I'm still trying to come to terms with it."

Harry shrugged again and offered everyone a sheepish smile.

"It's okay," Ash assured us. "And, believe it or not, you'd be surprised."

"We would?" I asked.

"We would?" Vance echoed.

Marshal Binson nodded.

"So, was there?" I asked.

"Was there what?" Ash asked.

"Was there anything left worth studying?" I quietly asked.

Ash shrugged and looked back at the paperwork. "In this case, only partial remains have been found, starting with the victim's right hand. A couple of hikers stumbled across it last week."

"I assume the roommate's DNA was in the system already?" Vance asked. "That's how you were able to confirm the owner of the hand?"

Marshal Binson nodded and helped himself to a

slice of pizza.

"Correct. His name was Michael Jeter."

"Was Mr. Jeter a member of the Daredevils?" Jillian asked.

Ash nodded. "Yes, ma'am. He's our link to this thrill-seeker group. Since Jeter was a confirmed member, and he is a former roommate, then my 'asinine theory', as my superiors put it, has some merit."

"Asinine?" Harry repeated, snickering.

"My superiors aren't as convinced as I am that this is a viable lead," Ash admitted. "However, I know I'm right. Jerod is hiding here, in Pomme Valley."

"Among these Daredevils," Tori mused. She looked over at my fiancée and smiled. "What do you think, Jillian?"

"I'm not a fan of putting Zachary in danger ..."

"He won't be," Ash hastily interjected.

"... but I do think it might be good for him to get out of the house and do something fun."

"You make it sound like I'm nothing more than a hermit," I grumbled.

Jillian took my hand in hers. "Zachary, I haven't seen you smile in a while. I know you're uncomfortable about getting older."

"I personally think a shot or two of adrenaline is just what the doctor ordered," Tori added, as she grinned at her husband. "Vance, you have my blessing."

"Zack, come on, buddy," Vance pleaded. "Don't

make me do this thing by myself."

I automatically glanced over at Harry. "What do you say, amigo? Are you with us?"

Harry had already started shaking his head, even before I finished asking the question.

"Not this time, man. I'm needed around the house. What, with Jules expecting, there's more and more she can't do. I can't go off and leave her like that."

"She has help," Tori announced, as she looked to Jillian for affirmation. "We can keep an eye on her for you."

Certain his excuse would get him off the hook, Harry paled as he realized his carefully rehearsed excuse had failed.

"Now wait a minute," Harry protested. "I can't get involved with this. I mean, I have a practice to run, man!"

"Nice try," Julie told him. "Dr. Richards has proven she is more than capable of handling the clients. Besides, it's not like you're heading out of town."

Vance and I each gave Harry a grin. After making certain he wasn't being watched, Harry flipped us both the bird. Together, we turned to the marshal. I nervously cleared my throat.

"Umm, I guess we're in?"

Marshal Binson eyed the three ladies at the table and noticed the way their significant others were now in hushed conversations with them. None of them looked happy, he decided.

"I'm never gettin' married," Ash quietly vowed.

THREE

T his is a mistake of biblical proportions," a voice solemnly declared, on my right, three days later. "This is soooo gonna come back to bite us."

"You're already shooting this down?" Vance sourly asked, as he turned to look at the person sitting in the back seat of my Jeep. "Seriously, Harry, you need to lighten up before you give yourself a heart attack."

"Is that another jab at my weight?" Harry demanded.

Vance held up his hands in surrender. "Nothing of the sort. Lately, you seem to be wound really tight. This is our chance to relax. Live a little. We're here to have fun!"

"Says you," Harry hotly returned. "You and Zack are in decent shape, so of course you'll have a good time. Well, you, at least. Zack? He may not be in as good as shape as you, bro, but he's definitely better than me. Come on, man. Let's just blow this off and turn around to go home."

"Do you even know where we're going?" I

asked, as I tried valiantly to keep the anger from my voice. If I'd known Harry was going to act like a big baby, then maybe I wouldn't have lobbied so hard to get him to join Vance and me. "I think you might be surprised, pal."

"Of course, I know where we're going," Harry grumped. "We're meeting up with a bunch of teeny boppers to try and blend in with them, as though we're all going through mid-life crises."

"He is going through a mid-life crisis," I pointed out, as I looked over at Vance.

"Bite me, dude," my detective friend returned.

"I figured he's just worried about that Jerod guy," I added.

"Thank you!" Harry cried, as though he had been waiting hours for someone to bring up mention of the fugitive. "Not only will we be risking our own lives for some guy we don't even know, but now we could be sitting next to a freakin' mass murderer!"

"Seriously, Harry," I scolded. "You need to calm down. Switch to decaf, will you?"

Harry blinked at me. "Huh? I haven't had a cup of coffee in years."

I whistled. "You haven't? You sure sound like you have."

Vance sniffed the air, looked first at me, and then twisted around to look at Harry.

"Then why do I smell coffee? I know Zack doesn't drink it. I haven't had any today, so it's gotta be you, pal."

"Well, I might have had a couple of cappuccinos this morning," Harry confessed.

"Coffee, cappuccino, it's the same thing," Vance decided. "Look, we're here. Harry, are you feeling better now?"

We had just pulled up to one of Pomme Valley's lesser known bars, namely Red Barn Tavern, when Harry finally fell silent. The three of us leaned forward, which afforded us a better look. Granted, I have never stepped foot inside the place before, but you'd expect a place named after a barn to, well, look like a barn. What we saw, on first glance, was a building which was modeled after an old, worn down saloon one would expect to find in a ghost town. However, there was nothing vacant about this particular business.

The doors were wide open. Loud, thumping music reminiscent of what a giant's heartbeat must sound like pulsed through tiny, concealed speakers. Bright, welcoming lights flooded through the open doorway, beckoning passersby to step inside. Being situated next door to the post office, I would have expected there wouldn't have been much foot traffic. There simply were too many cars going in and out of the post office to warrant an approach on foot. However, that didn't stop the people clearly craving a drink, as there was a steady stream of patrons both coming and going, suggesting whatever this particular bar was serving, it was in high demand.

"Doesn't look too bad, right?" Vance said, as he

stepped out of the car. "May not look like much on the outside, but I'm sure the inside is nice."

"Have either of you ever stepped foot in there, man?" Harry asked, as the three of us approached the front entry. "I haven't."

"Me, either," Vance admitted.

"What are you worried about?" I asked, as I frowned at Harry. "It's a bar. How bad could it be if these Daredevils choose to meet at a tavern?"

Harry shrugged. "True. You're right. Sorry, bro. I didn't mean to be such a downer. Come on. Let's see what this place has to offer."

We walked through the open doorway and came to an immediate stop. The place was crammed full of people. There were no available tables, the bar was standing room only, and there were several streams of people steadily walking from one end of the counter to another, looking for an opening.

Every single one of them, and I do mean everyone, stopped what they were doing, paused their conversation, and even hesitated in mid-drink to stare at us as though we were each wearing ski masks and brandishing weapons. I should also point out that everyone looked to be in their twenties, and not one of those young bastards had a gray hair on their heads. That meant that I was officially the oldest guy there.

"Does anyone else think we've got the wrong place?" I quietly asked my friends.

Harry wordlessly raised his hand. Vance

pushed it down and brushed by me, on his way to the bar. As luck would have it, three people decided they'd had enough and departed. The three of us quickly took their spots. After we placed our drink order—beer for me and Vance and a lite beer for Harry—I slowly inspected our surroundings.

I don't know what any of us were expecting, but for me, this wasn't it. We're supposed to be meeting the Daredevils, but how in the world are we expected to carry on a conversation? The pulsating music was so loud that I felt the fillings in my teeth rattle. Just then, I felt a tap on my shoulder.

"Are you Zack Anderson?"

I turned to see a young, six and a half foot tall blonde Adonis who was so ripped he could have easily have given Chris Hemsworth a run for his money as Thor. The guy had shoulder-length blonde hair, was dressed in jeans and a tee shirt, and had tattoos covering both arms. If I didn't feel out of place before, then I sure as hell did now.

"Er, yeah, that's me. Are you Dean?"

The guy took my hand in his and shook it with bone-crushing force.

"Dean Babcock. I'm chairman of the Dysfunctional Daredevils. Pleased to meet you, Zack. Are these the two friends you said would be accompanying you?"

I shrugged. "Old fogeys stick together."

"You can stick something, all right," Vance grumbled. He held out a hand. "Vance Samuelson.

For the record, these two are older than I am."

Dean grinned and looked over at Harry.

"Harrison Watt. You can call me Harry. Do you really have club meetings here? Isn't it kinda loud, bro?"

Our new friend shook his head, leaned past me to place an order with the bartender, and then waited companionably for his drink to be made.

"It is rather loud in here," Dean admitted. "You don't want to hang out in here for too long. It can cause tinnitus."

"It can cause what?" Vance asked.

"Tinnitus," Dean repeated. He tapped his ears. "Ringing in the ears? It's not good for you." The bartender slid a bottle over to him. Our new friend took his bottle and indicated the three of us should grab our drinks and follow him. "Come on. You should meet the rest of the gang."

"Where are we going?" Vance asked, as we noticed Dean was now heading for the door.

"It's too damn loud in here," Dean explained, as we all headed outside. The music could still be heard, but at least my eardrums were no longer bleeding. "I can't think when it's that loud."

"Then why bother meeting here?" Vance curiously asked.

Dean held up his bottle. "Red Barn makes some of the best beer this side of the Rockies. They're microbrews, in case you're wondering. Most of our gang had never tried one before joining our club. Once they did, they were hooked. So, whenever we meet up, we stop by here first in order to get our drinks. Only then will we head to Sarah's."

Harry's face split into a wide grin. "Sarah's? As in, Sarah's Pizza Parlor? Now we're talkin', man!"

Dean nodded. "I know, right? I know they're fairly new in town, having opened earlier in the year. But I have to tell you, they have the best damn pizza in town."

"I'll drink to that," I nodded, and I did. "We were there just a few days ago."

"I can probably talk the guys into going to another place, if you prefer," Dean companionably said. "But, seeing how this is the second Wednesday of the month, you three are just in time."

All three of us shook our heads.

"I think we're all good," I said, which earned me nods of approval from Vance and Harry.

The walk to the pizza parlor was only about two blocks west. Dean held the door for us as we stepped foot inside and were instantly assailed by some heavenly aromas. My stomach decided to rumble just then.

"Was that yours or mine?" Vance asked, with a grin.

"Mine, I think."

Dean checked his watch. "Not bad. We're only ten minutes late. The gang should be here by now.

He led us to one of two separate rooms, which, according to the placard next to the door, were available for private bookings. The three of us followed Dean and found seats near the end of the table. However, before any of us could reach for our chairs, the dozen or so people already gathered around the table ceased their conversations and looked up at us as though we had just stepped foot into the wrong bar. A few seconds of uncomfortable silence followed, before a young, swarthy guy with a very prominent five o'clock shadow, sitting on the opposite side of the table, cleared his throat.

"Thor? Are these the guys?"

Thor? The members of this group called their leader Thor? Hadn't I just made a mental reference to the Norse god when I first clapped eyes on Dean Babcock? It was all I could do to keep my face comfortably parked in neutral.

"Allow me to make the introductions, Yeti," Dean casually said, raising his voice. "Everyone, this is Zack, Harry, and Vance. Guys? Let me introduce you to the club. As you've just heard, on the opposite side all the way on the end is Yeti."

The dark-skinned guy gave us a two-fingered salute.

"Yeti?" I softly asked.

"The dude's as hairy as a sasquatch," Dean chuckled, under his breath. "His real name is Patrick Zanten, but no one calls him that. He's my vice-chair."

I nodded. "Got it."

"Sitting next to Yeti is TooTall."

A gaunt, skinny guy stood up to shake our hands. As TooTall stood, all three of us ended up having to crane our necks to look up at the guy. Here was someone who definitely lived up to his name. He looked to be late twenties, had impeccably styled hair, and was wearing a polo shirt and khakis. For some reason, the presence of this guy made me feel a little better. I think it was because he looked like he was out of place here, sitting amidst these scruffy-looking, tattoo-wearing outdoor adventurists.

"I'm Billy Madison. You can call me TooTall, if you'd like. Everyone here does."

"Damn, dude!" Harry breathed in amazement, as his gaze traveled up TooTall's body to land on his face. "They weren't kidding, were they? If you don't mind me askin', bro, how tall are you?"

"I'm six-ten." TooTall responded, almost sheepishly. "I've always been the tallest one in the room."

"Sit down, TooTall," Dean instructed.

Well, I'd better make that Thor. If I was going to refer to Billy as TooTall, then I should address the entire group by their monikers. Was I the only one who thought it was silly as hell for a group of adults to call themselves by these absurd nicknames?

TooTall hastily sat, as though he had just been scolded by a teacher. Next to him was a young, African-American girl who had to have at least three diamond studded earrings in each ear. She was wearing a black tank top, a red and black leather jacket, black ripped shorts, and black combat boots. Her hair was short and dark, and currently in messy waves. The girl fixed us with a rather intense gaze, and that's when I noticed she had one of those tattoo sleeves covering her left arm, but whereas I'm used to seeing multiple images jammed together, this tattoo looked to be of a single image. Whatever it was, it wrapped around her entire arm. I also noticed she had some type of scar over her right eye. From a Daredevil excursion?

"Next to TooTall is Cecilia ..."

"Dagger," the girl interrupted, with a frown.

"... Dagger," Thor continued, as he gestured at the girl, who immediately pushed away from the table and stood up. "Believe it or not, she's the most efficient postal carrier you will have ever seen."

"Pleased to meet you, gramps" the girl quipped, as she shook hands with me. I noticed she had striking green eyes. Colored contacts? She repeated the gesture to the other two, but I couldn't help but notice she didn't repeat the comment.

Dagger's grip was surprisingly strong for someone of her size. And by that, I should point out that she looked to be less than five feet tall. I was nowhere close to matching TooTall in height, yet next to Dagger here, I felt like the Jolly Green Giant.

"Oh, I like her," Vance decided, as he turned to give me a thumbs-up.

"It's nice that we finally get some old people in here," Dagger continued, as she sank back down in her seat. "It'll help even things out some."

Vance's smile jumped off his face to land squarely on mine. I felt I should say something, to address being called *gramps*, but I didn't have to. Out of the corner of my eye, I could see Harry was itching to say something.

"Who're you calling old, chica?" he demanded.

"You," Dagger calmly responded. "Look at the three of you. Are you, or are you not, old enough to be my father?"

I slapped a hand over my heart and pretended someone had just shoved a knife through it.

"Oh, she striketh straight to the heart with that quip," I moaned, and immediately grabbed the table for support, as though I was in danger of losing my balance. Then I checked for a pulse on my arm. "But … I still live! Clearly, my pacemaker doth taketh the brunt of her attack."

Dagger snorted as she covered her mouth. She grinned at me.

"You're pretty cool …"

I nudged Vance in the ribs. "Did you hear that? Huh? Huh??"

"… for an old guy."

Vance nudged me back. "Yep, loud and clear, pal."

Thor then stepped behind the next person at the table, who was a pasty, sickly-looking guy who I'm pretty sure had spent less than an hour outside in the last year. He was wearing an un-adorned black shirt and black jeans. The young man rose to his feet and offered me a limp hand to shake. Unfortunately, it was cold and clammy. I had half a mind to recommend the daily usage of a hand gripper to build up his grip strength. No guy should have a handshake as weak as that one.

"This is Techie," Thor said, as he slapped a hand on each of Techie's shoulders and gave it a firm shake. "He single-handedly keeps all our electronics in good working order. And, he's an all-around whiz on a computer."

That explained the pale complexion. I was pretty sure I was right. This guy sat behind a computer for the vast majority of his day.

"Caleb Gyserman," Techie said, as he shook my hand and looked up at me. "Pleased to meet you."

"Likewise," I returned, looking down. Damn, this dude was short!

"And here," Thor announced, as he raised his voice to thunderous levels, "we have probably one of the most important people in the room. I give you ... Patch."

Patch? Vance, Harry and I shared a quick look together. This guy was important? Enough to have it shouted to the whole restaurant? Hell, the guy in question looked embarrassed to find himself at the center of attention. He was a good-looking kid in his twenties, who had curly brown hair and hazel eyes. What surprised me the most, though, was when he stood up, the top of his head didn't clear my shoulder. He couldn't have been more than five and a half feet tall. Aside from TooTall, what was with this group? Was everyone shorter than five-six?

I noticed Vance's eyes had narrowed. Was he thinking that, perhaps, this was Jerod in disguise? However, in the blink of an eye, the skeptical look was gone and Vance was thrusting out his hand to make the introductions for us.

"Patch here is our resident doc," Thor explained.

"I'm actually a registered nurse," Patch admitted. "I've had to patch up a few of our members on more than one occasion, so 'Patch' stuck."

"Next to Patch is Jitters," Thor continued, as he pointed at the woman on Patch's left. "So named 'cause she thinks everything is a conspiracy and I've never seen her calm down. Like, ever."

"If you knew what I know," Jitters mumbled, keeping her eyes fixed on the table, "you'd be worried, too."

"Then, on this side, we have Hippie ..."

A young guy wearing a blue jumpsuit nodded at us. It was easy to see how Hippie got his name. He looked as though he belonged in a '70s sitcom, with his long, feathery black hair and thick walrus moustache.

"... Jafo ..."

The next guy stood up. Finally! We have another tall guy! In fact, he looked as tall as I was, which was an even six feet. Unlike most of the others, Jafo here looked to be in fantastic shape and sported a healthy tan. This was someone I'd expect to find in a group like this. Jafo shook hands with the three of us and promptly sat.

"... C2 ..."

Yet another short white guy stood up. This one, I decided, had a strong boy-next-door vibe about him. He was good-looking, wearing a smile, and when compared to the rest of the group, the most approachable. He took my hand and gave it a firm shake.

"Caleb Brissel. Nice to meet you."

"Why do they call you C2?" Vance curiously asked.

C2 turned to point at Techie.

"His real name is Caleb, too. I'm the second Caleb, so that makes me ..."

"C2," Harry finished for him. "Makes sense, bro."

"On C2's right is none other than HQ," Thor continued.

I looked at the girl Thor was referring to and had to stop myself from shaking my head. This girl was wearing a hot pink crop top, white coveralls which ended just above her knees, and calf-high black leather boots. I have no idea how to describe her hair color, as I could see that it had been dyed blonde, only I could also see that the tips of the right-hand pigtail was red, and the left was pink.

I looked helplessly at Vance, who could only shrug. And Harry? Well, his expression mirrored my own. We really didn't know what the hell we were looking at.

The girl scrambled to her feet and thrust out her hand.

"Pleased to meetcha."

"Can I ask you something?" I hesitantly inquired after I had shaken the proffered hand. "HQ? Aside from headquarters, what is that short for? Your initials?"

The girl happily nodded. "You betcha!"

She promptly sat.

"I can see you have no idea who she's modeling herself after," Thor whispered. "Harley Quinn? From Suicide Squad? You know, the Joker's frequent lover and accomplice?"

I nodded. "Sure. Okay."

Thor grinned. "Still don't have a clue, do you?"

All three of us shook our heads no.

"You can Google it later. Now, finally, our last member is … care to guess?"

I looked at the last person at the table. I could tell from her facial features that she was Asian, only she had to be wearing some fairly extensive makeup since her skin was paper white, and we're talking white-as-snow white. She was wearing a long-sleeved black dress, accented with white collar and cuffs. Her long black hair had been braided, and was hanging nearly halfway down her back. I took one look at the girl and smiled.

"Wednesday?"

The girl flashed me a dazzling smile, something

which Wednesday Addams would never do. She nodded excitedly and pumped my hand.

"You're right! Oh, I'm so glad I pulled off the look. It's nice to meet you, Vance."

"I'm Zack," I corrected. I then pointed at my two companions. "He's Vance, and Harry is over there, on my right."

"I do hope you three are going to join our club," Wednesday gushed. "We haven't had any new members in quite some time."

"And why is that?" I curiously asked.

"She's kidding, of course," Thor hastily interrupted. He threw an arm around my shoulders and guided me to an empty seat. Vance and Harry followed close behind. "Take a seat guys, and welcome to the Dysfunctional Daredevils!"

Harry held up a hand. "I gotta ask, bro. What makes you guys dysfunctional?"

Thor smiled and held out his hands in an open gesture, indicating everyone at the table. "You tell me, Harry."

"Dysfunctional means not working properly."

"And it also means deviating from the norms of typical social behavior," Thor added, as he winked at the members of his group.

There was a collective whoop of approval, along with several whistles.

"Have you decided yet?" C2 asked.

Thor nodded and began pacing along the length of the table.

"Now that we've all met them, I do believe it's

time to come up with their appropriate Daredevil names." Thor stepped behind me and gripped my shoulders tightly, giving me a slight shake as he did so. "I happen to know that Zack, here, is the owner of Lentari Cellars. Therefore, I'd like to extend a warm welcome to Bacchus!"

I couldn't stop myself from grinning. Bacchus? The Roman god of wine? I could get on board with that. Vance and Harry were nodding, so I was at least grateful I didn't have to explain to them they were naming me after a mythological god.

Thor stepped over to Harry.

"I'm told you're the town vet, Dr. Watt. I guess if I had pets, I would've known that. Sorry, I don't. Anyway, your name will be Doolittle."

Vance and I both snorted with laughter while Harry shook his head with exasperation.

"What about him?" I asked, as he pointed at Vance.

"What does he do?" Yeti wanted to know.

Vance shrugged. "I work for the police department."

This had the effect of quieting the room.

"You a cop, aintcha?" Dagger accused.

Vance nodded. "Detective, actually."

Thor nodded knowingly and a broad grin appeared on his face.

"Oh, lord," Vance moaned. "Let's hear it."

"Fellow Daredevils, I give you Clouseau!"

"Oh, shit," Vance grumbled. "Seriously? You can't come up with a better name than that?"

Both Harry and I had to look away. However, based on the age of this young crowd, we had a sea of confused faces staring blankly at us.

"Who's Clouseau?" HQ naively asked. "I've never heard of him."

This, however, surprised Vance.

"What? Are you serious? Chief Inspector Jacque Clouseau? From the movies?"

"Which movie?" HQ wanted to know.

"I just can't," Vance said, as he looked helplessly at me.

"It's from the old Pink Panther movies," I helpfully supplied.

"I thought that was a cartoon," Techie said, puzzled. "There was literally a pink panther, and he was always being chased by this guy with a magnifying glass. Is that who you're talking about?"

"Google it," I smugly told Techie.

Unsurprisingly, he whipped out his phone to do just that.

"Now that we've all met the new recruits, it's time to go over our next excursion," Thor said, pausing only long enough for several Sarah's Pizza Parlor employees to set a number of pizzas on the table before us. Once they left, Thor continued. "I know you three are very new to the group, and usually I like to get to know you better before we go out and do anything, but we've been planning this trip for a while now, and we're all looking forward to it."

"Looking forward to what?" I wanted to know. "A trip? Where are you guys going?"

"We," Thor corrected, with a grin, "are all going rafting!"

"White water rafting?" Vance carefully asked.

"That's right, Clouseau," Thor said. "That's the beauty of this trip. We don't have far to go."

"We're going rafting on the Rascal, aren't we?" Harry gleefully added.

Vance and I both turned to look incredulously at our friend.

"Hey, I've always wanted to try it, man," Harry confessed.

"Please say you'll come with us," HQ implored, causing both me and Vance to look over at her. "Rafting is perfectly safe ..."

"... with the appropriate gear," Patch interrupted.

"... and the right guide," TooTall added.

"It's perfectly safe," HQ repeated, as a frown appeared on her lovely face, "and so much fun!"

"I've never been white-water rafting," I admitted to the room. "Does the Rascal River have enough rapids to make it worthwhile? I am no expert, but the stretches I've seen from the highway make it look fairly calm."

Thor nodded. "Oh, don't worry about that. Most of Rascal River has Class II rapids. It's great for first timers."

I immediately zeroed in on the one word that had leapt out at me.

"Most? Did you say, *most*? What the hell is that supposed to mean?"

Thor shrugged. "Well, if you want to get technical, there are a few Class III rapids, and one Class IV drop."

There was an audible clunk on my right as Vance hastily placed his drink on the table.

"D-drop? What kind of drop?"

"You can get out beforehand," Thor assured us. "In all the years I've rafted that river, never once has anyone who's gone through it had a problem. Trust me, it isn't that bad."

"Still plannin' on going with us, gramps?" Dagger smirked.

I wasn't about to be shown up by some damn teeny-bopper, which explained why my head was nodding even before Dagger had finished asking her question.

"Sounds like a day in the park," I assured the girl.

Dagger grinned at me again, finished her pizza, and then pushed away from the table.

"I've gotta run. My shift starts at five. See you Saturday at seven, Thor."

"We'll be there, Dag. Take care."

During the next twenty minutes, the rest of the group finished their pizza and did the same. Only when it was just the three of us, after TooTall had left, did Thor look up from his pizza. He singled out Vance and frowned.

"I know you're a cop. I knew it as soon as I saw

your name."

"Then why didn't you say something?" Vance asked, curiously. "Did you not want the others to know?"

"I wanted to make sure I wasn't being investigated."

Vance leaned forward and rested his elbows on the table. "You think I'm investigating you?"

I shook my head. "He isn't. Do you want to know why we're really here?"

Alarmed, Vance looked over at me.

Thor nodded. "Wouldn't you?"

I hooked a thumb at my detective friend and chuckled. "Mid-life crisis. He's turning forty this year."

Thor visibly relaxed. "Oh. Of all the things I was expecting to hear, that wasn't it."

"Since we're all being so honest," Vance began, "I think I should tell you that I am aware of the sky-diving accident that befell your club."

Thor solemnly nodded. "I kinda figured you did."

Vance sighed. "I hate to admit it, but Zack is right. I think I am going through a mid-life crisis. Harry and Zack are just trying to get me through it."

Thor was all smiles.

"Well, you've come to the right place, buddy boy. Trust me, on next Saturday? You're gonna forget all about turning the big 4-0!"

Well, for once, Thor wasn't wrong.

FOUR

H ow the hell did I let you talk me into this, man? I could be back home, on my couch, with a beer in my ... whoa! Jeeeezus! It's cold! You didn't say it'd be cold!"

"We're on the Rascal River!" Vance shouted, as our raft dipped low and another surge of water splashed over the edge, coating all of us with a fine mist. "This water is runoff from the mountains. Think it's the tropics up there?"

I couldn't help but smile. Here I was, in my forties, sitting on a rubber raft, while traveling down Rascal River in Southwest Oregon. I turned around in my seat to look at the rapidly disappearing shoreline. Jillian was there, holding two leashes, and waving at me. Sherlock, the little putz, was still head-tilting me, as though he wasn't sure why a grown man would venture out onto the water like this. After that first splash of water had hit me square in the face, I had to admit, I was having doubts.

I was gripping an oar with one hand and holding on to the raft's outside line with the other. For those who don't know, an outside line is a safety rope running along the outside of the boat, designed to allow people to cling to it in case you ended up falling overboard, or as the rafters would say, going for a swim. Sitting on my right was PV detective extraordinaire, Vance Samuelson. And behind him? Town veterinarian, Harry Watt, who at the moment, was whining like a little kid.

I glanced to my right as yet another wave hit our raft head-on, which resulted in a huge spray of water hitting Vance and me so hard that it felt as though we had been slapped. Vance stifled a curse and gripped his oar tightly in his hands. For the record, I should point out that he wasn't holding on to the outside line like Harry and I were. I could only assume Vance had more faith in the river rat hired to guide us safely down the river than I did. I do have to admit something, though. Vance did appear to be having the time of his life. If I was going to be honest, then I'll have to admit that I was, too. As for Harry? Well, I can't speak for the third member of our group, but based on the number of expletives coming from the next row back, Harry was most certainly regretting his decision to accompany us.

It might have something to do with attire. Sure, it was gorgeous outside, and I'm sure I could have gotten away with dressing in swim trunks, a tee shirt, and a pair of old sneakers. However, on a tip from one of the Daredevils, Techie, I believe, we were advised to wear wetsuits. Now, I've had the misfortune of wearing a wetsuit before, when I renewed my open water certification earlier in the year. Trust me when I say that a wetsuit magnifies every flaw you've got. However, I dropped all objections when I felt the temperature of the water. That's when Jillian had suggested shorty wetsuits. They were just as snug and form-fitting as the full-sized version, only these 2.5mm neoprene suits ended about four to six inches above the knees.

Harry had taken one look at the snug, form-fitting wetsuits and immediately shot them down.

"You two will look okay in those," Harry had told us. "Do you know what I'd look like if I put one of those on?"

"A person wearing a wetsuit?" Vance wryly suggested.

Harry shook his head. "Not even close. Haven't you ever seen someone wearing something so tight that, if they were to bend over, they'd probably bust a seam? That'd be me, man. I already know how I'd look, and that's not something I want to put on display."

"I thought you said you were on a diet," Vance argued.

Harry held his arms away from his side.

"Clearly, it's working wonders, right? Losing weight has always been difficult, bro. It's a sore subject. The only other thing I'll say is that you won't catch me wearing one of those."

Well, since putting the kibosh on our choice of

attire, Harry had instead elected to wear a simple t-shirt and a pair of shorts that looked like they were made of the same material as sweatpants. What kind of swimming trunks were those? Who in their right mind would want to wear something like that onto a boat? I mean, Harry had to know he was gonna get wet. Ever wear wet sweatpants? It wasn't pleasant.

I lost track of how many times we were soaked by waves crashing over the boat. After the most recent, I turned to look at Harry, looking miserable in his soaked clothes. If only he would have listened to us. For that matter, if only he would have listened to Julie, his wife. Even she could see that he was not going to have a good time should he stick with his fashion choices.

"No one is gonna care what you look like," I had pleaded, less than fifteen minutes before we pushed off from shore. "It's not too late to change into a bathing suit. Julie even said she brought one along."

"This'll be fine, bro," Harry assured me. "I don't plan on falling overboard, and this is comfy, so it'll work."

One look at Harry's face was all it took to see that he was regretting his choices. Oh, well. I tried.

Commotion in my peripheral vision attracted my attention. Quickly verifying that our own raft was in no danger, I glanced to my left and saw an identical raft, similarly loaded with passengers. I checked to my right and confirmed another raft was there, albeit farther upstream.

I guess I should tell you there were three rafts in our excursion. Thor was in the first boat, with what he deemed as the intermediate rafters. That meant the raft was holding four other members besides our fearless leader. The third raft had been reserved for the professionals only. They were the ones, I'm told, who were planning on hitting every single rapid on the river, including the dangerous drop-off we had learned about earlier in the week.

Thanks, but no thanks. I do believe I will watch the proceedings from the safety of the shore, thank you very much.

The three boats in our outing were holding six people each. Our raft, which was number two, held the three of us, along with two other Daredevils who weren't too savvy with this type of excursion, either. Vance and I were in the front row of the raft, with Techie and Harry directly behind us. In the last row was C2 and our guide, a nice—but firm—older gentleman by the name of Mick. Apparently, if you've been deemed a *noob* in the eyes of Thor, you were relegated to the kiddie raft.

The first raft held our exalted trip leader, Thor, TooTall, Dagger, HQ, Jafo, and another guide. Aptly named river rats, the guides typically sit in the back and instruct when (and how) to paddle. Thor and his crew were deftly leading the way down the river, as if they'd done it hundreds of times. Well, chances are, they have. Anyway, to make matters worse, the bastards were rowing

in perfect harmony, as though they were compet-
ing in an Olympic rowing event. Thankfully, Thor
must have given orders not to ditch the rest of us,
'cause every so often, all six members of the raft
would jam their oars into the water at the same
time and keep them there, immobile. It had the
effect of slowing their raft considerably.

Bringing up the rear was raft number three.
This was a larger raft, with an extra row in it. The
people using this particular raft were the elitist
jerks, led by Yeti, who apparently knew what they
were doing. Included in their ranks were Patch,
Hippie, Wednesday, and Jitters. Their guide was an
older guy by the name of Jason, who was sitting
in the back row. I remember thinking, when we
were introduced to our guides, that Jason looked
familiar, as though I had seen him somewhere in
town before, but damned if I could remember
where. Sitting by himself, directly in the next row
up, was Patch. I can only assume that, since they
were planning to hit every single rapid there was,
including the Class IV drop, that the boat needed
to be a little bit bigger. I later learned that this particular raft was deemed a sterny, which meant the
guide was sitting in the back and would occasionally use his two longer-than-normal oars for extra
power.

To say that I was glad I wasn't part of that
group would be a severe understatement. Lost in
my thoughts, I didn't see the river narrow, which
meant the current had picked up. Thankfully, our

guide did.

"Look alive, ladies," Mick snapped, as he jabbed his oar deep into the water and kept it steady. The raft immediately turned to the left, which brought us out of the drift we were experiencing. "Lateral, twelve o'clock."

"What's a lateral?" Harry quietly asked.

Vance pointed straight ahead.

"The river just got narrower, pal. Look at the water. We're moving faster now."

Mick nodded. "Precisely. Stay sharp. We gotta get the bow pointing straight ahead at all times. You don't want to hit a lat going in sideways. Left side, oars in. Stroke. I said left side only, ladies. Now, stroke!"

True to Mick's word, our speed picked up. With our guide shouting orders, we kept our raft pointing in the right direction. Being on the left, I ended up paddling whenever we were told to, and Harry? He tried several times to paddle, but since he was sitting on the right, got a handful of water dumped down his back by our irritated guide.

"Pay attention, dude," I hissed at Harry. "Paddle only when you're told."

"I'm so done with this," Harry groaned miserably.

The next thing I knew, we were rocketing down the river. Hoots and hollers sounded from the first and the third boats. Were any of us, in the kiddie raft, making a sound? Nope. Not one of us uttered a peep. I think all five of us were wondering the same thing: if we pee ourselves with fright, would enough water make it into the boat to wash the incriminating evidence away?

Just as quickly as it had appeared, the banks of the shore widened once again, which reduced our speed considerably. In fact, the stretch of river we were on was almost devoid of rapids altogether. The river was wide, calm, and clear, allowing us to see the riverbed below. Strangely enough, the first raft was here, and they were pointed straight at us, which meant they had deliberately turned their boat around. Plus, they weren't moving. Why?

"What's going on?" Vance wanted to know. "Why aren't they moving?"

"I wanna know why they are pointed our way," Harry added.

"It's proving time," Mick announced, sporting a huge grin on his face. "I love watchin' these things. It's why I sign up to lead these expeditions."

Mick angled our raft so that it headed for Thor's, and when we were within a dozen or so feet, he thrust his oar into the water to arrest our momentum. After a few minutes, with the three of us sharing confused looks with one another, the third raft arrived. They pulled up alongside us and tied their raft to ours. However, Thor's raft remained where it was, floating serenely in the water.

"I've got a bad feeling about this," Harry muttered, as the three of us watched Thor reach down into the raft and pull out an inflated inner tube.

HQ, wearing a bright, neon pink PFD (that's personal flotation device for those of you who may be rafting-impaired), said something to Thor and then stood up on shaky legs. Within moments, she had pulled out a second inner tube and had passed it to our trip leader. A third tube was tossed over from Yeti's raft.

"What are they doing?" Harry asked, perplexed.

"It's time to see if you lot deserve to be among the Daredevils," Mick announced, overhearing the question.

"How?" I asked, as I turned in my seat.

Mick pointed at Thor, who was busy attaching ropes to the inner tubes. Once the three 42-inch inner tubes were securely fastened together, Thor tied one end of the rope to his raft, and then flung the three tubes and the leftover rope over to us. Mick caught the rope, attached it to our raft, and then gently pushed his paddle into the water. I felt our raft drift away from Thor's, but not before the rope tightened between our two boats.

As I sat there, staring at the three inner tubes that had been tied in place between our raft and the first, it dawned on me what our initiation must be. These sadistic SOBs were gonna make us try and get from one raft to the other, without getting our feet wet. What do they expect us to do? Crawl?? I mean, there's no way someone could walk across that, was there? If I tried something like that, then I'd go—face-first—into the water after my first step.

"This doesn't look good," Vance muttered, as he studied the floating inner tubes. "Are they thinking what I think they're thinking?"

I nodded. "Sure looks like it."

"There's no way in hell, man," Harry agreed.

"Gentlemen!" Thor called, raising his voice. The hoots and hollers automatically began. "It's time to separate the boys from the men. I give you our Daredevils tradition! Let's see who among you can walk between rafts without getting their feet wet."

"My feet are already wet," I quietly pointed out.

"There's no way in hell, bro," Harry said, raising his voice. He leaned over the raft's edge and studied the closest inner tube. "No one could make it across that. I think you came up with this just to have fun at our expense."

Thor grinned and then held two fingers to his mouth. Several sharp, piercing whistles sounded moments later. "Daredevils! Did you hear what Doolittle just said? He not only thinks we're doing this so we can have a laugh at their expense ..."

"... which he'd be right ..." I heard someone say. Several chuckles ensued.

"... but that no one is capable of beating this challenge," Thor was saying. "Fellow Daredevils, who'd like to prove Doolittle wrong?"

"I'll do it."

All eyes turned to Dagger. The young African-

American girl popped up on her seat, navigated her way to the front of the raft, where Thor was sitting, and straddled the outside edge of the raft, like I've seen professional rafters do. And, for the record, I have never seen a black-colored life jacket ever. In fact, it even had teeny tiny decorated skulls on it, the likes of which you'd find on items decorated for *Día de los Muertos*. I wonder how much that personalized PFD cost her.

"That's not fair," Harry complained. "Look at her, man! She's tiny! If there's anyone who could do it, then she'd be the one."

"Clearly, we need a second volunteer," Thor added. "Do we have any takers?"

Much to my surprise, TooTall raised his hand. Thor nodded approvingly. He and TooTall switched positions on the raft, allowing both contestants better access to the inner tube rope.

"Dagger, make us proud," Thor instructed. "Are you ready?"

Dagger nodded. "Bring it on."

Thor held out a hand. "Whenever you're ready."

I sat, mesmerized, as the scene unfolded in front of me. Dagger nimbly hopped off the raft and landed on the first inner tube. However, before her full weight could register, she was already moving. She quickly jumped to the next ring, and unwilling to break her stride, she leapt to the third and final ring. Allowing her momentum to carry her toward our raft, she threw herself at us. Or, more specifically, at me, since I was one of the closest people to the makeshift line.

Not wanting her to fall, I immediately reached out and caught the girl in my arms. Dagger instinctively threw her arms around me and waited a few moments, as if she couldn't believe she lucked out and made it to our raft. Now certain she knew she wasn't going for an unscheduled swim, she grinned up at me, released her death grip on my arms, and turned to wave at Thor in the other raft.

A chorus of cheers erupted.

"Way to go, Dagger!"

"We knew you could do it, Dag!"

"Nicely done!" Thor praised, from the first raft. "Did you see that, Doolittle? We wouldn't place obstacles before you if there wasn't a chance of winning."

Harry pointed at TooTall. "Hey, bro, I expected her to do it. She's tiny. Let's see how he does."

Thor turned to TooTall. "You're up, my friend. Don't let us down."

TooTall shrugged. "Piece of cake."

The young man swung his long legs over the raft, set them on the first tube, and stood up. Now, I will say that I expected the tall thrill-seeker to go ass-first into the water, but much to my surprise, he managed to keep his feet. But, as skinny as he was, his weight was more than what the tube could keep above water. He started to sink.

Not wasting any time, TooTall took several

giant steps and, before any of us knew it, he was standing on the third tube and was about ready to hop aboard our raft. Unfortunately for him, a gust of wind appeared, bringing a welcome relief to the warmer weather. Unfortunately, it pushed our raft slightly out of position.

The raft shifted, the inner-tube-rope-thing-amajig lost its tautness, and down went TooTall, much to the delight of his fellow Daredevils.

"Almost made it that time, TooTall!" Yeti shouted, from the third raft.

TooTall surfaced, grinned up at us in the second raft and then, unconcerned, swam back to the first raft. Acting like this sort of thing happened to him all the time, TooTall pulled himself back in the raft and accepted the towel Thor was offering him. Thor then turned to face Harry and held out a hand, encouraging him to volunteer to go next.

"There's no way," Harry muttered, again.

My detective friend sighed heavily, "Let's get this over with. I'll go first."

Vance handed me his oar, swung his legs over the side of the raft, and looked at the closest floating tube.

"I think speed will be your friend," I quietly muttered.

"I was thinking the same thing," Vance whispered back. "I've seen this sort of thing on those ninja-obstacle-course shows. Okay, wish me luck, pal."

Vance quickly stood up, flailed his arms as he

struggled to get his balance, and once it became certain he wasn't gonna get it, bolted for Thor's raft.

He almost made it. Kinda.

Vance's right foot slipped off the edge of the inner tube and into the tube's center. As a result, his foot caught on the upper rim of the second tube and propelled him forward. Poor Vance face-planted into the third tube and ended up doing a half belly-flop into the water.

The Daredevils roared with laughter. That, I'm sorry to say, included me and Harry.

Sputtering, Vance surfaced, and once he spotted our raft, swam back to it.

"You almost made it," I told him, as I pulled him into the raft. "You made it to the third tube. That's impressive, buddy!"

"An admirable attempt!" Thor announced. "Not bad for a beginner, Clouseau!"

Vance cringed as he heard his Daredevil name.

"Bacchus, are you ready?"

I sighed and then shrugged. "Why not? I'm just gonna forewarn you guys. I probably won't make it past the first tube."

Actually, I made it to the second. I'd like to say that I tripped up, the same as Vance, but again if I'm being honest, I'll say that I was trying to regain my balance. Then again, I don't think I ever had it to begin with. I ended up belly-flopping worse than Vance, much to the delight of my fellow Daredevils.

"Oh, this sucks," Harry moaned, as he realized it was now his turn. "I'm so going in."

Both Vance and I turned to look back at our friend, sitting behind us. Drops of water fell off our clothes and pooled on the raft's floor, in front of us. We both silently regarded our veterinarian friend.

"Let me guess," Harry said, as he looked from one unsympathetic face to the other. "Neither of you care."

"We both went in," Vance reminded him.

"And it wasn't very graceful," I pointed out.

Harry sighed, swung his legs over the raft's edge, and tentatively placed one of his feet on the toroid-shaped flotation device. He looked imploringly over at me and Vance, gritted his teeth, and took a deep breath.

"Go quick," Vance instructed. "If you stop to think about what to do next, then you're going swimming."

"Word," I added, which made the two of us snicker like schoolboys.

Harry quickly stood up, and took a step forward. But, before he could, the inner tube jetted out from under his feet, sending him ass-first straight down. The tube, being tethered in place, quickly returned to its original place, which meant Harry's butt landed squarely in the tube's hole. Such was the force of Harry's fall that it actually wedged him in the tube, nice and tight.

Vance whistled with appreciation. "Would you look at that? He didn't get wet."

"Well, most of him, anyway," I corrected.

"Way to go, Doolittle!" someone praised.

"He didn't make it across!" another protested.

Mick carefully made his way over the raft's rows of seating until he was next to me. He quickly untied the line of inner tubes and pulled the raft next to Harry. Between the two of us, we were able to pull Harry into the raft, only much to everyone's delight—and Harry's dismay—the inner tube remained wedged on his rear end.

"I'm afraid you'll have to get that one off yourself, mate," Mick told him, as he made his way to his seat at the back of the raft. He watched Dagger nimbly jump back to the first raft. "Thor, you ready to get underway?"

Thor nodded. "Absolutely. That was a fantastic showing, guys."

"No one but Dagger completed the challenge," I pointed out.

Thor shrugged. "I wasn't interested in seeing you beat it, only that you tried to beat it. Besides, there are only a few of us who have successfully made it across. One of these days, I'm sure I finally will."

"Will what?" Harry demanded. "You mean, you haven't made it across, either?"

Thor grinned and leaned over the raft to untie the rope. Seeing that Mick had already untied the rope on our end, Thor began pulling in the inner tubes. He shook his head as he pulled up the first tube.

"Look at this thing! It won't hold a full-size adult."

I ended up laughing. I had to admit that it made me feel better, knowing that most of the Daredevils had been just as unsuccessful as we had been. That was when I heard it.

A woof.

My head jerked up and I started scanning the river bank. There, much to my chagrin, were the girls. Jillian had the dogs' leashes in one hand and a video recorder in the other. I groaned when I realized what that meant. Thor must have somehow sent word to our significant others that a prime Kodak moment would be happening, and where — naturally — it was going to take place.

Jerk.

"What's the matter?" Vance asked, as he handed me back my oar.

I pointed at the shore. "Don't look now, but our escapades have just been filmed."

Vance straightened, saw his wife and daughters waving at him, and smiled sheepishly. He gave a slight wave back before he grinned at me.

"Did you know they were going to be there?"

"Nope. If it wasn't for one of the dogs barking, I wouldn't have known to look."

"What's going on?" Harry asked, as we resumed our progress down the river.

Vance turned to point back at the river bank.

"The girls are back there. So are my kids and Zack's dogs. They filmed the whole thing, pal.

That should be good for a laugh later on."

"What?" Harry exclaimed, as he turned around to check for himself. "Julie never said she was going to be here!"

"Well, they are," I said. "Don't worry, buddy. There's nothing to worry about."

We were moving slowly enough on the river that I caught sight of Jillian and the rest of them casually pacing us along the riverbank. The only thing we could hear were a few muted conversations, which occasionally broke out in laughter. I then noticed Sherlock and Watson, only they weren't looking at me. They were looking at the raft behind us. What would be their interest in the third raft?

I turned in my seat to check on the progress of the 'professionals'. They were about fifty feet behind us, and were also lazily drifting along the river. I could tell that there were a few conversations taking place there, but I couldn't tell what was being said.

"Heads up, ladies," Mick announced. "The Rascal is waking back up!"

Our velocity increased as the river narrowed yet again. Swirling currents, choppy water, and some serious dips in the river lay dead ahead. I felt my pulse quicken and, without realizing it, a grin appeared on my face. I felt a nudge in my ribs and, after glancing over at Vance, saw that his face had a similar grin.

"Here we go!" Vance all but cried, as our raft hit

the first of the new rapids.

Down went our raft. Up went the water. It felt like I was in a water fight, and my opponents all had buckets of cold water to throw at me, and I had run out of ammo. Seriously, water was splashing at us from all directions. All three of us, I might add, were laughing hysterically, which, at times, would switch to screams of terror as our raft played pinball through the rapids.

"I thought you said there were only a few Class III rapids!" I said, as I turned to look back at our guide.

"Those were barely Class II," Mick informed me. "You wanna see a Class III? We're approaching one now. Better treat her nice, mates. She'll work you over if you don't."

For the next thirty seconds, I'm ashamed to say that I acted—and probably sounded—like a little girl as I saw what was waiting for us. This Class III rapid was nearly thirty feet long, had several dips, and one very narrow descent. I learned, later, that this particular rapid had several holes right next to each other. That meant there were a series of rocks where water would flow over it, and then drop down to the river below. As if that didn't sound bad enough, the water would then flow downstream and then back toward the falling water. Seriously, if you didn't know what you were doing, you could be in a world of hurt.

Thankfully, Mick was an experienced river rat. He skillfully jabbed his oar in various places as we were jostled by the rushing water to give the raft a gentle push here, and a not-so-subtle shove there. Somehow, and I don't know how, Mick prevented us from flipping over when it looked like we were about to, and he avoided getting a single drop of water on himself. As for the three of us? I'm told we sounded like we were riding a roller coaster, because every time our raft made any rapid movement—which was a lot—we all screamed like kids. Not to mention we were drenched. Our wetsuits? Definitely a wise choice. I could only wonder how Harry was coping with the cold water.

Still laughing like lunatics, Mick instructed us to paddle over to the closest shore. There, waiting for me, were Jillian and the dogs. Both Sherlock and Watson were whining and pulling on their leashes. When I finally made it over to them, I ended up having to spend a few minutes assuring my dogs that I was okay. The two of them kept nudging my arm up, as though I needed to give them more scratches behind their ears.

"I'm okay, guys. Thanks for the love."

Sherlock dropped into a playful crouch.

"Awwooooo!"

"He has not been a happy camper," Jillian told me, as she took my hand in hers. "Zachary! Your hand is freezing!"

"Well, the water is cold."

"Where are they going?" Jillian suddenly asked.

Vance, Tori, and his two daughters wandered close. Overhearing, they all turned to look back at the river. We watched as the third raft continued by us and disappeared around the bend. Harry and Julie then arrived.

"It's gotta be that Class IV drop-off Thor was talking about," Vance decided. He pointed at the rest of the Daredevils, who were in the process of following a dirt path west. "I'll bet that's where they are going. Come on. Want to watch 'em go over?"

"No one is going to get hurt, right?" Jillian cautiously asked.

"That raft has all the pros in it," I explained, as we followed Vance and his family down the path. Looking back, over my shoulder, I saw Harry and Julie following. "Class IV rapids can be really dangerous, so Thor said only a few of the group would be taking that monster on."

We arrived at the observation point. I stared, open-mouthed, at the obstacle my fellow Daredevils were about to hit. That was a rapid? From my vantage point, it looked like a thirty-foot drop! How could that possibly be construed as anything but lethal?

I followed Jillian over to the railing. Several signs had been posted, giving information about the Class IV rapid. Turns out I'm not a good judge of heights. My thirty-foot drop-off was actually less than a dozen feet. Still, it looked dangerous as hell.

"Here they come!" Tori exclaimed. "Oooo, I wouldn't want to be on that boat."

"Neither would I," Vance admitted.

We watched as the raft slowly approached. Number Three's guide was using both of the long oars, attached to his stern seat, to make constant corrections, in addition to jamming both of them in the water at various points in an effort to take the drop as carefully as possible. The five Daredevils sitting in the raft, Yeti, Jitters, Wednesday, Patch, and Hippie, were also expertly paddling the water. Sometimes only on one side, and other times both sides paddled in unison. And not one of them, I should add, looked to be concerned.

The raft's nose edged out, over the drop-off. With the guide shouting orders, the Daredevils withdrew their oars and allowed the raft to finally move forward. Every single person present— participants and observers—screamed with delight as the raft inched out over the drop-off. However, I noticed right away something didn't go as planned.

"She's gonna flip!" Thor cried.

The head of the Daredevils sprang forward, hurdled the safety railing, and rushed to the water's edge, just in time to see the raft's bow get pulled under. As a result, the raft slanted dangerously downward. The Daredevils' cries of delight quickly switched to screams of terror as the raft lost its balance and flipped over.

I took one look at the rapidly swirling water and handed the leashes back to Jillian. Next thing I know, I'm following Vance over the rail and hurrying to the water's edge. Thor had already unwound the rope he was wearing around his waist and was looking for a suitable place to tie it off. Catching sight of the two of us, he immediately handed me the end.

"Hold on to this! Both of you! Look, there's Yeti! Over here! Swim for it!"

Yeti's bedraggled form was pulled to the shore and then Thor single-handedly hoisted him out of the water. Vance grabbed Yeti's arm and pulled him further up the embankment. In this manner, we pulled out the rest of Daredevils as they surfaced, and then finally, the guide, Jason. Unfortunately, we were one 'Devil short.

"Where's Jitters?" Thor helplessly cried. "Who's got eyes on her?"

FIVE

The rhythmic thumping of helicopter blades had me glancing up. For the third time in the last ten minutes, a search helicopter flew over our heads as it slowly patrolled up and down the river. I sighed, looked down at both of my corgis, and kept walking downstream. Sherlock whined once, turned to Watson, and shook his collar to get her attention. Once she was looking his way, the inquisitive corgi actually gave his packmate a quick lick on the side of her face, as though he wanted to say he appreciated her presence.

The baying of a nearby pack of bloodhounds generated a few warning woofs from Sherlock. I quickly glanced across the river and located the second team of police dogs, searching the opposite riverbank. Hopeful that the hounds had picked up a scent, I pulled Sherlock and Watson to a stop. Unfortunately, the two bloodhounds must have thought the scent wasn't worth following and moved on.

"Think we're going to find her?" I quietly asked

Vance, who was walking alongside us.

Vance solemnly nodded. "I have no doubt that we will. However, I hope you realize this isn't going to be a rescue. No, this will be a recovery mission."

"I just want to know what happened to her," I said, carefully stepping around a section of the riverbank which looked as though it was ready to break away from the rest of the ground and drop into the river. "Do you think it was an accident?"

"I sure as hell hope it is," Vance gravely answered.

"But you think it isn't," I guessed.

Vance nodded. "This marks the second death to befall Thor and his gang. That can't be a coincidence, not when he tells me that no one in his club has ever had anything more severe than a bruised finger."

"I'm just glad there were several people present who filmed the entire thing," I said, a few minutes later. "I'm looking forward to reviewing the footage. Maybe we'll be able to see something?"

We heard a bloodhound baying in the distance. I swallowed nervously and eyed my detective friend. "I hope that doesn't mean what I think it means."

Vance whipped out his cell. "Let's find out. Detective Samuelson here. What … you have? Just now? I see. Where did you find her? Okay, send for the M.E. and have the scene techs go through everything that they can. I'm on my way. I'm guessing it'll take me around thirty minutes before I can get there. I ... what's that? No, I was helping the others search. Zack and I are upstream, and progress is ... yes, that Zack. Yes, Sherlock and Watson are here, as a matter of fact. No, we don't think it is murder ..."

"Yet," I quietly interrupted.

"We'll be there as soon as we can."

"At least they found her. Was she, er, in the water?"

"Of course she was, Zack. She fell off a raft. There was bound to be water."

"No," I said, shaking my head. "I was wondering if she was, er, found under the water?"

"What difference does it make?"

"Nothing, I guess. I was just wondering."

"Well, she was found, face-down, tangled up in several shrubs that were growing out over the water. We'll find out soon enough. Come on."

In actuality, it took us a bit longer than thirty minutes to retrace our steps, make it back to our cars, and then find the scene of the accident. I wasn't expecting to reconvene with Jillian. Turns out she and the girls had already gone home. Thankfully, my fiancée left me her SUV and hitched a ride with Tori and her two kids.

Vance gave me a speculative look as he noticed we were headed toward Jillian's SUV and not my Jeep. After a few moments, he snickered and shook his head.

"What?" I demanded.

My friend grinned at me. "Nothing."

Let me guess. You're probably thinking along the same lines as Vance, which means you probably believe …

a. Jillian and I are way too sappy, seeing how we now have keys to each other's cars.

b. We are two peas in a pod, and are clearly destined to be together.

c. We've both fallen head over heels for each other.

d. All of the above.

If you guessed 'd', then you're right. And do you know what? I'm perfectly happy with that. Jillian and I share a great many things in common. One thing we both like is …

Wow. Not the time or place. Sorry. I've said it many a time, and I'm sure I'll say it plenty more: I have a tendency to run off on a tangent. Back to the story.

Returning to Reality Land, Vance and I hurried to the parking lot. Vance noticed his sedan was missing and, correctly guessing Tori had taken it to take her and the kids home, immediately angled towards Jillian's SUV. I grabbed Sherlock, and Vance picked up Watson. Once both were sitting in the back seat, we hurriedly drove upriver, to the spot where poor Jitters' body had been found.

By the time we made it the five miles—by car —half of PV was already on the scene. Fire trucks, ambulances, and six of PV's seven police cars were parked alongside the road. Vance held up his badge as we exited the vehicle, which caused the approaching officer to spin on his heel and head back to his post. Vance strode forward to talk to the officer while I unloaded the dogs. Together, the three of us approached the perimeter cop, who waved us through.

"Where is she?" I wanted to know as the dogs and I pushed through the crowds of people milling about.

Vance pointed at a gurney several dozen feet away.

"Right over there. Come on. I'd like you and your secret weapons to do a drive by, if you will."

"I thought you said you guys don't suspect this to be a homicide?" I asked.

Vance shrugged. "I'm thinking it's not, but what could it hurt to check?"

Not fully expecting much, the dogs and I wandered by the gurney. Thankfully, a sheet had been laid out over Jitters' body, and I couldn't see anything. However, the instant we got within ten feet of the body, I'm sorry to say both dogs perked up. Sherlock came to a stop, which caused Watson to stop as well. Both dogs lifted their noses, sniffed the air, looked up at the body, and then turned to look back at me, as if I was somehow responsible for this tragedy.

"What the hell was that for?" I complained, as I frowned at both dogs. "I didn't do it."

Sherlock then lowered his snout to the ground, sniffed again, and just like that, he was off. Together, he and Watson pulled me back toward the river, but then angled upstream before we could reach the spot the body had been found. Seeing how we appeared to be following some type of game trail, and it definitely hadn't been created by someone as tall as me, I spent most of the time hunched over. Dense foliage and thorny shrubs threatened to tear my skin and clothes from all angles as I followed my two dogs farther upstream, and away from the public.

"Where are you going?" I heard Vance say, from somewhere behind me.

I pointed down at the dogs. "Beats the hell outta me. You and your damn ideas. This is all your fault. 'Just do a drive by,' you said. 'What harm could there be?' Well, the dogs took one look at the body and then they took off. Sherlock? This had better not be a wild goose chase, buddy."

Vance's cell rang just then. I pulled the dogs to a stop, but received a gentle push on my back from the detective.

"No, don't stop. I can multi-task. Detective Samuelson here. Chief Nelson! I didn't know it was you, sir! What number are you calling from? No, sir. You're correct. It doesn't matter. I'm glad you called. I ... what's that? Yes, sir, I realize I'm on vacation. I'm just helping with the search, that's all. I'm a member of the same group as the deceased. What's that? No, I'm no longer at the scene. I'm with our consultants. Yes, those consultants. Umm, that's yet to be determined, sir. The moment we find something, I'll let you know. Thank you, sir."

"No pressure there," I commented, as I continued to push my way through the brush and shrubs. Was it me, or were these shrubs growing closer? "Guys? You two might be fitting on this trail, but we're sure not. There had better be something at the end of this, that's all I'm telling you. Don't let us down."

"Talk to your dogs often?" Vance wryly asked, from behind me.

"All the time," I admitted. "You'd be surprised at how much they seem to understand. Hold up, Sherlock is finally slowing down. He ..."

"What is it?" Vance asked, after I had trailed off. "What do you see?"

"It's just a damn picnic area," I reported, as I pushed my way through the branches and into the small clearing. "There's nothing here but a picnic table and a small grill. What, are you smelling ... some leftover food?"

Vance immediately placed a hand on the side of the grill and shook his head.

"It's cold. This thing hasn't been lit for a long time. Zack? Give them some slack on their leashes. Let's see where they want to go."

Curious as to what the corgis had in mind, I let out the slack I had been holding. Both dogs, sensing they were given free rein to explore the area, headed straight for ... the trash can. I groaned as I leaned over to look inside the refuse bin.

"Whatcha got?" Vance eagerly inquired. "Tell me it's something good, buddy."

I gingerly lifted the trash can's lid and looked over at my friend.

"Not a damn thing, I'm afraid. Look, there are some leftovers from—I'm guessing—the last picnic which was held here. Hot dog wrappers, some half-eaten buns, and an open bag of chips."

"Are those the only things in there?"

I shook my head. "No. That was only the stuff on top. I mean, we have some candy wrappers, a few empty beer cans, and a couple of other things I can't identify. Sherlock? Watson? Is this what you wanted us to see? Or are you hungry?"

Vance snapped on a pair of latex gloves, reached inside the bin, and pulled out the hot dog wrapper, complete with dripping juice. Both dogs stared at it, transfixed. Vance groaned as he realized there wasn't anything we could use in the trash can and dropped the wrapper back inside the bin. He pulled out his cell, hurriedly punched in a number, and wandered off. From what I could overhear, he was reporting in to the chief, and I can only imagine the report he was spinning wasn't going to be good.

Glancing back at the trash bin and remembering all the times the dogs had led me to what I had originally thought of as worthless in the eyes of a case, I decided to document what we found. Pulling out my cell, I snapped some pictures of the various bits of trash I could see. Since I didn't have any gloves on me, I wasn't about to touch anything inside. Giving the trash bin a few good jostles, and taking several additional pictures as a few new bits of trash made their way to the top, I let the lid clang back in place. Gathering up the leashes, I gave them a gentle tug, indicating I wanted to follow Vance, who was now retracing his steps back to the accident scene.

Both dogs resisted. Sherlock let out a whine as he looked longingly at the trash can. Watson resisted, too, but only for a few moments. After a few seconds, she snorted, gave herself a good shake, and started off toward the trail. I swear it sounded like Sherlock sighed with disgust before he turned to follow the two of us back to civilization.

When will I learn to pay attention to the dogs? Had either of us been paying better attention, we could have saved ourselves a lot of time. But, more on that later.

By the time the four of us made it back to the scene, preliminary reports were suggesting that this was nothing more than an accident. However, wasn't that what they said about that poor, unfortunate sky diver from a few weeks ago? Didn't the authorities classify that as an accident, too? Could this Jerod person be responsible for both of these deaths?

I saw Vance talking with Thor, who—pardon the pun—looked like death warmed over. The Daredevils' illustrious leader had sunken eyes, a glazed expression on his face, and could barely form coherent sentences. Vance caught sight of the three of us and motioned us over.

"As I was saying," Vance continued, as he referenced his tiny notebook, "we are going to need contact information for everyone on that raft. By any chance, do you remember who was on it?"

Thor nodded desolately. After a few moments, he sighed. "I, uh, know there was six people on number three. In fact, there were six people on every raft. We do it for safety."

"6-6-6," I quietly breathed.

Vance's pen was poised just above the notepad. He quickly elbowed me in the stomach before nodding at Thor. "I'm ready. Who was on it?"

"Well, it was headed up by Yeti."

"Full name, please," Vance instructed, without looking up.

"Oh. Of course. Umm, Patrick 'Yeti' Zanten. Sitting next to him was Patch, er, I mean, Nate Hesterman."

As Thor began speaking, I could see some color return to his face.

"Second row had Joel 'Jafo' Kline and Lisa 'Jitters' Nordon. Then there was Darcy 'Wednesday' Addams in the third row."

Vance looked up. "Who was she sitting next to?"

"No one. She was by herself. Finally, just behind her—in the last row—was the guide, Jason."

"Full name please?" Vance asked, as he scribbled notes on his pad.

"Jason Johnson. We've used him before, including our last rafting trip. He did a fantastic job. Had impeccable references."

"Why did he have his own set of oars back there?" I wanted to know.

"Yeti and Jason led the pro raft," Thor explained. Now that he was talking, I could see that he was starting to look—and sound—like his former self. "Since the Daredevils who'd ride that raft would be navigating down David's Drop ..."

"Excuse me," Vance interrupted, looking up. "David's Drop? Is that the name of that Class IV rapid?"

Thor nodded. "Right."

"Not very original," I decided.

"Well, it was named after the first guy who lost his life on it," Thor nonchalantly told us. "It was what his family wanted."

"Someone else has died on it?" I asked, dumbfounded.

"A few," Thor told us.

"When was the last?" Vance wanted to know.

"Are you asking when David last claimed a life? Well, that'd be at least ten years ago. No one has had any problem with this river in ages."

"What do you think went wrong?" I asked. "What do you think happened to Jitters?"

"The medical examiner found water in her lungs," Vance answered, as he unfolded a handwritten sheet of paper from his back pocket. "Jack didn't find any signs of foul play, either. Of course, we won't know for certain until an autopsy is performed, but he feels confident enough to say that Jitters' death was nothing more than a horrific drowning accident."

"Jack?" Thor repeated, puzzled.

"Jack Spradlin," Vance said, nodding. "He's our M.E. He's been PV's medical examiner ever since we got an influx of dead bodies."

"What?" Thor incredulously repeated. "Dead bodies? What zombie apocalypse was this?"

Without missing a beat, my schmuck friend looked me straight in the eye and said, "I can't say for certain. When did you move in, Zack?"

"Oh, kiss my butt," I grumped.

"What'd I miss?" Thor asked.

Vance pointed at me, "Ever since he moved to town, it would seem we've had nothing but murder after murder. Before Zack moved here, this town hadn't seen a real-life murder for just over fifty years."

"You cannot attribute that to me," I scowled. "It's a coincidence."

"How long have you known each other?" Thor wanted to know.

"Oh, don't ask him that," I groaned.

Vance shrugged. "Ever since I first arrested him for murder, I guess."

"You were accused of murder?" Thor gasped.

"Accused, yes," I admitted, "but later proved innocent. It was just my bad luck to be in the wrong place at the wrong time."

Thor sighed and sank down on the closest rock which would serve as a chair.

"I'll have to close Daredevils."

"Look, pal," Vance slowly began, "I know it looks bad, but don't jump the gun. Let's find out what the official cause of death is before we make any rash decisions."

Thor ran his hands through his hair and groaned aloud.

"You don't understand. Our last excursion? Prior to this? It was skydiving. That's when we lost Hades."

"Hades?" I repeated.

"Right. Oh, sorry. That'd be James Thompson. There was a manic depressive if I ever saw one. It was why he joined up. Said he wanted a change of pace to cheer him up. Fat load of good that did him."

"What happened to him?" I wanted to know. "Did he pass out in mid-air and not open his chute? Or ... um, did his chute not open at all?"

"It was the latter," Thor confirmed. "That's a day I won't ever forget. Now, today will rank right up there with some of the worst of my life. What am I supposed to do?"

"Keep the Daredevils alive," a new voice suddenly announced. "In Jitters' honor. And Hades', for that matter."

We all turned to see the rest of the Daredevils, lined up as though they were posing for a picture, a dozen feet away. Yeti had taken several steps forward and looked as despondent as Thor. One by one, the rest of the Daredevils joined him, forming a semi-circle around us.

"You can't let this get you down, man," Yeti was saying. "It was an accident, nothing else. How could it not be? I mean, you should have seen Jason. He somehow leapt from the back of the raft to the front, and was almost able to keep the raft from tipping over. He's the one who single-handedly got us out of harm's way. I'm not ashamed to say this, but if it wasn't for him, then I think there'd be a few more fatalities on your hands."

"Without a doubt," Wednesday agreed, nodding.

"If you shut down the team now," Yeti continued, "then you admit you're letting your fear control your actions. Honestly? I've never thought of you as being someone who succumbs to their fear, Thor."

"That's two, Yeti," Thor quietly said. "Two of our members are gone."

"They were both accidents," Patch argued. "They weren't your fault. You'd be doing all Daredevils a disservice by disbanding us now."

"You're suggesting we carry on like nothing has happened?" Thor asked.

Yeti nodded, and then looked back at his fellow Daredevils to confirm. Every single one of them nodded back. I had to hand it to Thor. He was certainly heading up a loyal group.

"What about you two?" Thor asked, turning to us. "What do you think, Clouseau? You're the cop. What would you do?"

I softly snorted and had to look away. Vance gave a visible start, as though something in his line of sight had spooked him. It had the intended effect of making Thor turn to look behind him. The moment he did, Vance slugged me on the arm.

"Jerk," he hissed at me. "It's not that funny."

"Yeah, it is," I whispered back, between chuckles.

Several Daredevils sniggered behind me, having witnessed the exchange. Thor turned back around and faced Vance with an expectant look on his face. My detective friend eventually shrugged.

"I guess what I would do, if you're asking my opinion, is to carry on under the impression that what happened was just an accident."

Hoots and hollers sounded from behind us.

"That is," Vance hastily continued, "as long as the official cause of death is ruled as accidental drowning."

Thor eventually nodded.

"That's fair. Daredevils? Did you hear that? We're still here!"

The hoots and hollers turned into thunderous cheer.

"In honor of Jitters, may our next adventure be just as thrilling!"

"N-next adventure?" I sputtered. "You're going on another one? Already?"

"Well, yeah! Isn't that what Clouseau suggested? We carry on as though nothing has happened."

"Thor?" Yeti called out. "Could I get your opinion on something?"

The leader of the Daredevils nodded. "Of course."

I noticed that the rest of the group hovered close by, as though they'd be able to hear what was transpiring between the two leaders. I was about ready to wander over when Vance tapped me on my shoulder and inclined his head in the opposite direction. Curious, I followed my friend as he put some distance between us and the 'Devils.

"What's up?"

"I think we have a problem," Vance began.

"Of course we have a problem," I said, scowling. "It looks like they're planning on having another excursion, and unless we bail out and look like wimps in the process, we're gonna have to go through with it."

"I'm not worried about that," Vance told me.

"Well, I am, amigo!" I turned to point at the ambulance, which was just pulling away. "I'm worried that it could be one of us in there next."

"We won't be, pal."

"How can you be sure? Level with me. Do you think this is a homicide or an accident?"

"Based on everything I've seen before me, I'm leaning toward accident."

"Fine, if you're not worried about the threat of

imminent death, then what's the problem?"

Vance pulled out his notebook and flipped a few pages until he found what he was looking for.

"I thought for certain this death was Jerod's doing."

"So did I," I admitted. "You must have thought Jerod was responsible."

Vance nodded. "Of course I did. We have a serial killer here hiding in PV. Their last two excursions each end up getting one of their members killed?" Vance sighed and rubbed his temple. "I thought this had Jerod written all over it. My problem is, based on everyone's account of what they saw, our suspect should be on boat three, right?"

"I follow your logic."

"Well, according to the Daredevils, the people on raft number three are Yeti, Patch, Wednesday, Hippie, and Jitters."

"And Jason, the guide," I added.

"Right. Zack, none of those people fit Jerod's profile. I mean, obviously, Jitters and Wednesday are female, so they're out. That leaves Yeti, Patch, and Hippie. We already know it can't be the guide: he's too old. The problem is, none of the other three match what we were told Jerod should look like."

Realizing Vance was right, I frowned. Were we wrong? Was Jerod one of those three in disguise? If Jitters' death was a homicide, then that meant Jerod had to be on that raft. How else could he have pulled that off?

"It's settled!" Thor's voice announced. "We have decided on our next adventure. Bacchus, Clouseau, would you care to hear what you'll be doing next?"

"I seriously don't like my Daredevil name," Vance darkly muttered.

I was doing my damnedest to keep from laughing. As soon as Thor announced his plan, trust me, my laughter died in my throat. In fact, I could feel that all the blood had rushed out of my face.

"Guys and gals, we're going bungee jumping!"

SIX

Can you believe we're really gonna do this? I mean, holy cow, I've always wanted to try this. Haven't you wanted to try?"

"Try what?" Vance demanded. "Jumping off a perfectly good bridge and hope to hell the rope is going to hold? Are you insane?"

I grinned at my friend. "Having second thoughts there, buddy-boy?"

"Brilliant deduction, Holmes. What do you do for an encore?"

Have you ever noticed when you want something to happen, that it'll take its sweet time getting there? And, conversely, when you want to keep a certain deadline from approaching, then it flies toward you at warp speed? Such was the case for us. As you've no doubt noticed, I may have sounded willing to trust a group of complete strangers and allow myself to fall from a seriously tall height. You'll soon see that, however, when I finally made it up there, and I was staring at that drop-off up close, I was going to have an abrupt change of heart.

I should probably catch you up. Vance and I were currently in Bend, which is just under two hundred miles from PV. If you were to look at a map of Oregon, you'd see that Bend lies in the central part of the state. As for how long it takes to drive here? Well, with me driving, it was about three hours. If Jillian would have driven? I'm positive that not only would we have made it with time to spare, we'd also have time to grab a bite to eat, stop by a rest area to freshen up, catch the latest movie, and so on. When that woman gets out on the open road, and is allowed to play whatever she wants on the stereo—as loud as she wants—then she has a tendency to develop one helluva lead foot.

"You two are going to be just fine," a third voice assured me.

Not wanting to be left behind, Marshal Ash Binson had expressed a desire to tag along. But, since the rest of the Daredevils had taken a chartered bus out to the spot Thor had chosen, and in case Jerod Jones happened to be familiar with what the marshal was driving, Ash had asked if he could hitch a ride with us. Once I pointed out that he'd have to ride in the back seat with the dogs, his face lit up like the 4th of July. Turns out the good marshal really loves dogs. Vance was prepared to ride with us, too, until Tori announced she and their two girls, Victoria and Tiffany, would like to watch their dad jump off a bridge. So, they ended up taking their own car and following us.

Even though our road trip had only lasted three hours, we ended up stopping for potty breaks and snack runs on three different occasions. I still wasn't complaining, though. One thing I've learned that I really enjoy, especially when Jillian was present, was taking a road trip. On top of which, I was surprised to discover I was secretly enjoying my time with the Daredevils. Yes, they were all younger than me, but darned if they weren't full of life. They lived each day as though it would be their last. They loved to experience new thrills, and much to my surprise, me, too. However, that was a little tidbit I was doing my best to keep under wraps. I don't need anyone accusing me of having a mid-life crisis, too.

"You seem to be enjoying your time with these people," Jillian announced, which had the added effect of making me jump with surprise. "Are you okay, Zachary? I didn't mean to startle you."

"No, I'm good. Thanks."

"Mm-hmm. Perhaps you could slow down a bit?"

"Huh?"

"Your speed. From where I'm sitting, it looks as though you're doing ninety."

Surprised, I checked my speed. Yep. Eighty-eight miles an hour. How long had I been doing that?

"You're enjoying yourself, aren't you?"

I looked over at my fiancée and took her hand

in mine.

"I am. I don't remember enjoying road trips as much as I do now. You, the dogs, and the open countryside. It can't get any better than that."

Jillian brought our clasped hands up to her face and gave my hand a gentle kiss.

"That's sweet, Zachary. But, that's not what I mean and you know it. So, back to the original question. You're enjoying your time with these people, aren't you?"

I sighed and nodded sheepishly.

"Guilty as charged. There's something about living life to the fullest that appeals. I'm not sure why. I've never been that way before."

"There's nothing wrong with doing activities that you enjoy," Jillian patiently explained. "I never would have pegged you for an adrenaline junkie."

"That's because I'm not," I laughed. "Let me be crystal clear about something. I'm not one hundred percent on board with what we're about to do."

"Bungee jumping," Jillian thoughtfully said. "I'm not too surprised. It's a dangerous sport. Are you actually going to go through with this?"

"It's actually safer than you might realize," Ash mentioned from the back seat.

I could see that his head was down, and he was looking at something on his phone.

"Have you ever been?" I asked him.

"What? Bungee jumping? Hell no."

"But ... but you just said it was perfectly safe!" I stammered.

"Oh, they claim it is, and I've seen first-hand how strong those ropes are," Ash said. He still hadn't looked up from his phone.

"I'm sensing there's a *but* in there," Jillian said, suppressing a giggle.

Ash nodded. "There is. I'm not about to put my life in the hands of total strangers. I don't care how safe it is."

"And you expect us to follow through with this after that little comment?" I demanded.

Ash shrugged. "Some people handle certain situations better. Personally? I have acrophobia. I looked up this place your God of Thunder picked out. Peter Skene Ogden Scenic Park. Have you heard about where you'll be jumping? It's one of the highest jumps in North America. It's definitely the highest in Oregon."

My mouth was suddenly bone dry.

"Uh, er, h-how high is it?" I nervously asked.

"Two hundred fifty feet."

I visibly relaxed. "Two fifty? That's it? Whew. For some reason, I thought it'd be way higher than that."

"Just wait until you're on the bridge, looking down," Jillian teased. "I'll bet you'll be singing a different tune."

She hit the nail on the head. As Vance and I joined our fellow enthusiasts, we got our first look at the bridge where we'd be performing our jump.

This was two hundred fifty feet? Good god! The Peter Skene Ogden Scenic Park (that's a mouthful, isn't it?) bridge looked as though it was thousands of feet off the ground. We were gonna jump off that?? Harry had the right idea by bugging out on us. And, seeing how we're on the subject, since when was Harry the smartest one of the group?

"That looks really high, daddy," a young female voice said, from my left.

I turned to see Vance, Tori, and their two daughters approach. The oldest one, Victoria, was thirteen years old, had straight brown hair, and was wearing a pink tee shirt and white shorts. She leaned over the rail and gasped as she looked down at the ground far below.

"What do you say, princess," Vance began, as he came up behind his eldest. "Want to go with me?"

"Oh, absolutely not!" Victoria cried. "No way! There's no way I could do that!"

"What about you, Tiff?" Vance asked, as he turned to his youngest daughter. She was a shorter, blonde version of Victoria. "Want to go with me and Zack?"

"You're jumping off that?" Tiffany hesitantly asked. She was eleven, wearing a cobalt blue shirt advertising some boy band, and a yellow skirt. "No, thank you."

"I think they have the right idea," I quietly muttered, as I stepped up beside my friend.

Vance grinned. "Having second thoughts?"

"And you're not? Dude, look how high we are!"

"I haven't looked yet," Vance confided. "And I don't want to. If I do, then I have a feeling I'm gonna pull a Harry and chicken out."

"I think he's the smart one here," I said. "And if you ever repeat that, I'll deny it, even under the most heinous of torture."

Vance chuckled as I fell into step behind him. He paused long enough to kiss his wife—I did the same for Jillian—and then we all headed out to join our fellow Daredevils at the jumping platform set up around the halfway point on the bridge. Several other groups of people were also there, and about every ten minutes or so, another (un)lucky individual would leap off the bridge, much to the delight of the onlookers.

"Sure you don't want to look?" I teased Vance.

My detective friend had his head down and quickly shook his head. "Absolutely not."

"What's your plan? Are you going to keep your eyes closed the entire time?"

"They're not closed now."

Just then, I heard a set of matching warning woofs. Surprised, I looked back at the dogs, who were both trotting alongside Jillian. Sherlock and Watson were both fixated on the small group of people gathering near the jumping platform. The problem was, I couldn't tell who they were barking at. Was Jerod there, in disguise? If so, who was he? And how were we going to tell him apart from the other potential candidates?

Sighing, I pulled out my phone and snapped a

few shots. I'd have to check through the photos later.

A quick glance over at Jillian confirmed she and I were on the same page, meaning she had her phone out and was sending a message to Ash. She was typing as she walked, which I figured must mean Ash would already know about the corgis' behavior by now. Since Marshal Binson was not a master of disguise, like all the reports claimed Jerod was, Ash had elected to remain inside the car. Armed with a pair of high-powered binoculars, I'm sure he was watching us at this exact moment.

We arrived at the halfway point on the bridge, and joined up with the rest of the adrenaline knuckleheads. I leaned out over the guard rail and studied the flowing river far below. There was no way we could only be two hundred fifty feet up in the air, could we? I mean, it looked like we were easily ten times higher than that. At that time, both of Vance's daughters arrived by my side. The oldest looked down at the ground far below and then turned to give me a speculative stare.

"Are you really going to do this, Mr. Anderson?"

I shook my head. "I have a feeling, Ms. Victoria, that the only way you'll see my fat butt falling off that bridge is if I'm pushed."

Both girls erupted into laughter.

Right about then, Vance made the mistake of joining us. Without realizing what he was doing, he looked out into open air and saw for himself just how high up we really were. I heard my friend suck in his breath and mutter a curse.

"You just said a bad word," Tiffany accused her father. "You owe the swear jar five dollars!"

"One buck per infraction," Vance dryly corrected.

"But you tried to hide it by not fessing up," Victoria corrected. "Didn't you say that deception causes the fee to increase five-fold?"

Giving the young teenager an appreciative look, I glanced over at my friend. Vance shook his head and pulled out his wallet. "Here, young lady." And then, to me, he added, "Just when you think your kids aren't paying attention to you."

"When money is involved, they're always listening," I helpfully pointed out.

"Daredevils!" Thor's voice announced, causing everyone around us to fall silent. "Welcome! I'm glad you're here. As you can see, we have a treat for you! We've arranged our jump to happen right here, above the Peter Skene Ogden scenic park! Who's excited to be here?"

A chorus of cheers went up. None, I might add, could be heard coming from our little group. I heard another warning woof from Sherlock. Both Vance and I stared down at the little corgi, but he refused to look at us. My tri-colored boy only had eyes for the Daredevils. That had to mean something, didn't it?

"This is the part where I ask for volunteers to go first," Thor announced, "but in this case, since we have two new members, we don't have to. Bacchus, you have the honor of going first!"

I felt the color drain from my face as I realized these people fully expected me to be dropped off a flippin' bridge. People began cheering and clapping me on the back as I hesitantly stepped forward. Vance, the little turd, was all smiles. Jillian took my hands in hers and squeezed them encouragingly.

"You can do this, Zachary. I believe in you."

"Whatever happened to 'No, this is too dangerous and I don't want you to go,'? I mean, I don't know if I can do this."

A strong, firm hand appeared on my shoulder and squeezed.

"Sure you can," Thor said, coming up on my right. "You're here, aren't you? You want to experience all life has to offer, don't you?"

I remained, transfixed, at the railing's edge.

"Come on. They've got to get you suited up and go over some safety protocols with you."

I looked at my hands. I was gripping the rail so tightly that my knuckles were white. "Tell that to them," I told Thor. "I don't think they want me to go."

In a daze, I allowed myself to be pulled over to the group of strangers, who immediately began outfitting me in a special harness. A man and a woman, both looking to be about my age, calmly —and professionally—started strapping things on me while going through the unsurprisingly long list of bungee jumping Dos and Don'ts.

"Don't try to fall feet first," the man was saying, as he adjusted several straps on my harness. "For obvious reasons, that can get awkward."

"Do you really have to throw that disclaimer in there?" I incredulously asked.

"I wish we didn't, but we have to," the woman sadly added, as she strapped a bright yellow helmet to my head.

I shuddered as I thought about what must have happened. "That'll leave a mark."

"And then some," the guy agreed.

He snapped matching straps around my thighs and then pulled my shoulder straps down and fastened it to some type of oval ring. The guy caught me staring at it and grinned.

"You're a big boy, so I upgraded your carabiner for you."

"Uh, thanks?" I stammered. "Care to tell me what a carabiner is and what it does?"

The male operator leaned forward and tapped the flattened metal ring hooked to my chest straps.

"It's this metal clip right here. If you press this side in here, do you see how it opens? And, based on its design, you can also see that no amount of force will open it from the inside-out."

I saw a tiny '25kn' etched onto the ring.

"What's that?" I wanted to know.

"That? It's your kilonewton rating. This baby is rated at 25 kilonewtons. I usually use 21 for most jumps."

"You're calling me a lard-butt, aren't you?"

The guy snorted with laughter.

"We don't take any chances. A 21kn-rated carabiner will hold you, but I would personally feel better with something stronger. What was your weight again? Two fifty?"

"More or less," I said, cringing as my weight was publicly announced. "How much will this hold?"

"Oh, stop fretting," the woman chided. "It's held bigger people than you, darling. Sit here. That's good. Now, have you gone?"

"Have I gone? No. Clearly, I'm still here."

Idiots. Where else would I be? The woman smiled patronizingly at me before continuing.

"I mean, have you gone to the bathroom yet?"

Oh.

"I did at the last gas station. Why?"

"We just recommend you don't jump on a full bladder," the man explained.

"Afraid I'll pee myself, is that it?" I scoffed.

"Think about it, buddy," the man told me. "If your drop is underway, and you release your bladder, where do you think your pee is going to go? Think about which way you'll be pointing, and what gravity will be doing to you."

"Oh. Eww!"

"There's a $75 cleaning fee if you soil the harness," the woman casually informed me, as if grown adults peeing themselves happened on a daily basis. Then again, it probably did for them.

"I'm pretty sure I'll be good." I hope, I mentally added.

The man excitedly smacked his hands together and began vigorously rubbing them.

"I think that's it. You ready?"

What? Was I ready for what? That was when I discovered what the husband-and-wife team had been doing. The entire time this exchange was taking place, they were surreptitiously edging me closer and closer to the jump point. Once I realized what they were doing, I slammed on the brakes and gripped the handy dandy rails that were within arm's reach. I waggled a finger at the two of them and frowned.

"Oh, hell no! Damn, you two are good. You almost got me."

"Listen, pal," the man began. "If you don't want to make the jump, that's fine. However, seeing how close you are to the drop-off, at least let me put the rope on you, in case you develop a case of vertigo and topple forward, okay? I don't want any deaths on my hands. It looks very bad on the reports I'd have to fill out."

"You're serious?" I demanded, as I leaned over to check my ankles. "The rope isn't even attached?"

Sneaky bastards. They were just waiting for me to look at my feet. Why? Because, when I leaned forward (I was sitting on the deck), I inadvertently let go of the rail so as to better look at my trussed-up ankles. Well, the clever jerk was waiting. As soon as I shifted my weight to my other hip, I felt a hand on my back and suddenly discovered the ground had disappeared.

"Have a great time!" I heard the man cheerfully shout down at me, as I dropped away from the platform.

That's the last thing I heard before a series of screams, pleas, and curses drowned everything else out. That sneaky, two-timing, silver-tongued bastard had pushed me! The only thing I could hope for is that I could hold on to my dignity and not embarrass myself on the way down. Well, as you could probably tell from the 'screams, pleas, and curses' from above, that didn't happen. In fact, I was pretty sure that, if Victoria and Tiffany had been listening, I was going to end up owing their swear jar at least $50, if not more.

On and on I fell. Granted, what felt like eons only ended up lasting less than six seconds. One second, I was at the top of the bridge, doubting my life choices. The next? I was bobbing up and down under a bridge, like an oversized yoyo. Upside down, mind you. Moments later, a second cord was dropped down beside me and, after I clicked it into place, I was hoisted back up to the platform.

The Daredevils were there, all whooping and hollering. Congratulations were given, and I even didn't mind being called gramps by a few of them. I guess the vast majority of them thought I'd chicken out. And, let's be honest here, I almost did.

"Nicely done, mate," the male operator said, as he started unbuckling me from my harness.

"You pushed me," I accused, as I unbuckled my safety helmet and pulled it off.

The male operator held up his hands in surrender.

"That wasn't me, pal. Do you know how much trouble we would be in if one of us actually did?"

"Then who did?" I wanted to know.

"Do you regret going?" the female operator asked.

I shrugged and eventually shook my head. "Not really. I don't think I'd ever do it again, but at least I can say that I did it."

"So, you're proud you did it, is that it?" the woman clarified.

"I guess you could say that."

"That's good to hear, 'cause I'm the one who pushed you."

I whipped my head around to stare at the wife part of the husband-and-wife team. "What about what he just said? About the amount of trouble you could be in if one of you pushed a jumper off the platform?"

The woman shrugged. "What can I say? Money talks."

"Money talks," I repeated. I looked over at Vance, who happened to be talking with his family. Laughing and joking, by the way. "Did my friend over there pay you to do it?"

"I don't know what you're talking about," the

woman said, but gave me a barely perceptible nod of her head.

"Thank you. That's all I needed to know."

So ... he thinks he's funny, does he?

"Looking for retribution?" the woman quietly asked me. She had a grin on her face and I could tell she had something in mind.

"Absolutely. Whatcha got for me?"

"For $79.99, Max here will suit up and jump alongside your friend."

"How is that retribution?" I wanted to know.

"He'll have a video camera on his helmet and will record your friend's reactions all the way down."

"Sold! Do it."

The male operator—Max—gave a hearty laugh and opened a nearby blue duffel bag. He pulled out his own personal harness and began putting it on. Laugh at me, will you? Let's see how your face looks on the big screen, amigo. This will be totally worth it.

"Hey, no hard feelings, right?"

I looked over at Vance, who was slowly walking my way with his family. I thought about how silly I must have looked on my own drop, and what Vance would inevitably look like as well, and grinned. I thrust out a hand.

"None whatsoever. Hope you have fun, amigo!"

Vance's smile vanished in the blink of an eye.

"What did you do?"

"What are you talking about?" I asked. I had to

make sure I kept my face comfortably parked in neutral.

"Something's up. I want to know what you did."

"What who did?" Tori asked, overhearing Vance's statement.

My detective friend pointed an accusatory finger at me.

"Him. I want to know what he did."

"Why do you think Zack did something?" Tori asked, confused. "Wait. Did you do something to him?"

"Well ..."

"Vance Edison Samuelson. What did you do?"

"She just middle-named him," I chortled, as I sidled up next to Jillian. Both dogs nuzzled my legs, as though each suspected I had suffered some type of trauma and wanted to see for themselves I was okay. Now that I think about it, I guess what I just did was traumatic.

"It was nothing, really," Vance stammered. "I might have paid a few bucks to the platform organizers to give Zack a push if he started showing signs he might back out."

Tori looked horrified. She gave me an apologetic look, but before she could say anything, I winked at her. Vance's wife immediately drew up straight, looked at me, over at Jillian, and then slowly looked over at her husband. Vance, meanwhile, was staring at the ground, so he missed the interchange. Tori looked back at me and gave me an inquiring look. I mimicked an old-fashioned, hand-crank video camera and then pointed at Vance. Tori's eyes widened, and Jillian suppressed a giggle. Just like that, Tori dropped all objections. She knew I had somehow arranged for Vance's drop to be recorded.

"Well, what's done is done," she eventually said.

Vance whirled on her. "Okay, what? What's going on? Since when have you let me off the hook that easily?"

The husband-and-wife team approached and started getting Vance ready for his drop. Thankfully, the ever-observant detective didn't notice that there was a second suited-up person on the platform besides him. Tori appeared on Jillian's right, whispered something to her, and then pointed at the camera on Max's helmet. Jillian nodded, then tapped me on the shoulder.

"Is he going to record Vance's jump?"

I nodded. "All the way down, yep."

"Does Vance know?"

"Nope."

"Tori is going to love this."

"Everyone is going to love this," I corrected. "Especially when I invite everyone over and play it on the big screen."

"Zachary, you wouldn't!" my fiancée protested.

"I can and I will, my dear."

Five minutes later, the rope had been attached to Vance's ankles and he had been positioned at the jump point, with his legs dangling out into open air. Vance turned to look at his family as his girls started shouting encouragement.

"Good luck, daddy!" Tiffany called out.

"Have fun, daddy!" Victoria yelled at the same time.

"See on you the big screen!" I shouted from the observing area, nearly a dozen feet away.

Vance blinked with confusion. "Huh? What was that?"

I waved a dismissive hand and watched as both Vance and Max dropped off at the same time. While not able to see too much of my friend from my vantage point, I could certainly hear him. Like me, he yelled, cussed, screamed, and cussed a little more. But, in his defense, he did execute the jump under his own steam and didn't need any prodding from bribed officials.

Once Vance had been reeled back in, like an oversized trout on a fishing pole, and unbuckled from his harness, we moved our respective families off the bridge and onto the public viewing area back on terra firma. Picnic tables were set every few feet, so we selected two that were close together and claimed them for our own. That was when Vance and I started comparing notes.

"I couldn't even form coherent thoughts until I bounced the first time," Vance admitted.

"From the sounds of it, you were second-guessing yourself," I told my friend. "However, I'm not one to argue. I screamed like a little girl all the way down. It was all I could do not to pee myself."

That comment earned me a few giggles from Vance's kids.

"Did you get that spiel, too, about when you went to the bathroom last?" Vance asked. "Talk about lousy timing. There I was, trussed up and unable to move, and I get asked about bathroom breaks. Hey, what was with that guy doing a drop from the second line?"

I waved a dismissive hand. "Oh, it was nothing."

"You're up to something."

"Maybe."

Sherlock and Watson went into Clydesdale mode and forcefully pulled Jillian up to Vance's side. It was Vance's turn to get the corgi bill of health, seeing how they had heard him scream and shout moments earlier. Jillian handed me the leashes as she sat beside me at the table. In the distance, we could hear the hoots and hollers of the rest of the Daredevils as they each took their turn.

"Do you have any regrets?" Jillian asked, as she clasped my hand in hers.

"About doing that? No, not really. I mean, I'm not gonna do it again, thank you very much. But, I am glad I did it. Why? Did you want to try it?"

"Oh, heavens no," Jillian laughed, shaking her head. "That's not for me."

"What's the matter?" I teased. "Haven't you ever wanted to … what are the dogs doing?"

The two of us looked over at Sherlock and Watson, who were straining at the end of their leashes while firing off warning woofs. Both, I might add, were staring back at the bridge. More specifically, they were staring at the group of people who were still there, waiting their turn.

"What's going on?" Jillian wanted to know. "Can you see anything?"

I shook my head. "No. It's too far away to … hang on. I'm going to go grab Ash's binoculars."

"What if he's using them?"

"It'll only be for a little bit. I really don't want to walk all the way back out on that bridge to see what's going on."

Less than five minutes later, I was back, holding a very expensive set of field binoculars.

"I'm surprised he let you borrow them," Jillian said.

"It really wasn't that difficult. I gave him a brief history of how the two dogs work, with regard to cases. Once I told them that they expressed interest in the jumpers, Ash felt that perhaps Jerod was out on the bridge. He practically thrust these things into my hands."

Jillian's phone beeped. We both looked down at the display and saw that Ash had sent a message, wanting to know if I had spotted anything.

"Tell him I'm looking now," I reported, as I adjusted the focusing rings on the binoculars.

Jillian tapped the message into her phone. Then, she looked up at me.

"Well? What's going on?"

"Not much. Another Daredevil is preparing to jump. I can't tell who it is."

"It's C2," a friendly voice said, from behind me.

Properly spooked, Sherlock fired off a warning woof before turning around. Jafo was there, holding out a hand to the dogs. Sherlock and Watson sniffed once, gave the owner of the hand a few more warning woofs, and then returned their attention to the bridge. Jafo slid his lanky frame into the seat opposite me at the table and grinned.

"It's a helluva lot of fun, isn't it?"

"Now that I've done it," I began, "I can safely say I don't need to do it again."

"We'll get you properly motivated yet," Jafo vowed, as he turned his attention to the bridge. "C2 is up, and looks like he's ready to jump."

"How can you tell from this distance?" Jillian wanted to know.

"He's the only one wearing a black t-shirt with a red skull on the front and back."

I put the binoculars back up to my eyes and studied the distant figure. Jafo was right. The next jumper had a black shirt, and I could see parts of it were red.

Sherlock woofed again. I gave the corgi a pat on his head and smiled apologetically at my fellow Daredevil.

"Don't worry about him. Some people just get him riled up, even though he's way the hell over there, and we're here. Go figure."

"What do you know about C2?" Vance casually

asked. "Has he made many jumps?"

"Not much," Jafo confirmed. "As for jumps, from what I hear, he's done more than any of us. But, the majority of them were done elsewhere. C2 has only been with the company for about two months now. He's even newer than me."

"You're new, too?" I asked, surprised.

"I've been a Daredevil for just over three months" Jafo confirmed.

"If you don't mind," Jillian began, "could I ask you about your name? Jafo? Is that short for something?"

Jafo grinned and nodded. "It's an acronym, actually. It stands for Just Another Effin' Observer."

"Clever," I chuckled. I held out a hand. "Zack Anderson."

Jafo took my hand and gave it a firm shake. "Joel Kline. Pleased to meet you, Zack."

"This is my fiancée, Jillian. And over there? That's Sherlock and Watson."

"They're corgis, aren't they?" Jafo wanted to know. "I've seen the breed before. Cute dogs."

"Yep," I nodded. "Sherlock? Watson? I know you've already met him, but I'd like you both to come here. Wait. Why are you still woofing at the jumpers? Is C2 still there? He hasn't jumped yet, has he?"

Jillian took the binoculars and held them up to her eyes.

"He's still there," she confirmed. "Perhaps there's a problem?"

"Probably got cold feet," I decided. "It just doesn't make any sense. Why now? If he's a veteran jumper, then why would this throw him for a loop?"

"He's probably arguing with the guy running the platform," Jafo guessed. "C2 seems to be angry with just about everyone. I'm not sure why."

"What do you know about him?" I asked, genuinely curious. "Aside from having a history of jumping, that is."

Jafo shrugged. "Well, his real name is Caleb Brissel. From what I can tell, he appears to be a loner. I don't think he has any friends. I've personally invited him and a few other Daredevils out for drinks, or dinner, and C2 is always the one who turns me down."

"C2 is the computer tech, right?" I asked.

"He's *a* computer tech, just not *the* computer tech. That distinction belongs to Techie."

"Got it," I nodded. "What does C2 do?"

Jafo shrugged. "He maintains all the Daredevils' social media accounts. He always seems to have some type of gizmo in his hand."

Caleb Brissel, I thought to myself. He was the right age and the right height. He knows his way around a computer, and more than likely, uses it to keep tabs on anyone who might be looking for him. This was someone who would make a damn fine suspect for a disguised murderer, desperate to remain hidden.

I made eye contact with Jillian, hopeful that I

could persuade her to send a message to Ash, only I didn't have to. My fiancée already had her phone out and was in the process of tapping out a message. Just then, Jafo stood up and held out his hand again.

"I'm next. Guess I should start getting prepared. I'll see you three later."

"Wouldn't that be something if Jafo was our Jerod," Vance idly remarked.

I was already shaking my head. "There's no way. Ash said that Jerod was only five foot six tall. Jafo is, what, at least six feet?"

Vance shrugged. "True. I will say, though, that I'm really leaning towards this C2 guy. I mean, look at the dogs. Neither of them have taken their eyes off of him."

"C2 wasn't on the third raft," I pointed out. "He wasn't even in the first. He was in ours, buddy. Don't you remember? He was seated next to Harry."

"Oh. Damn, I didn't remember that. Well, perhaps Jerod had help?"

"There are no known associates," I said, lowering my voice. "As far as we know, he doesn't know anyone else in town."

"Besides that roommate," Vance interjected.

"Who is dead," I reminded him.

"True. As I was saying, there are no known ..."

A piercing scream split the air. The three of us gasped with alarm and leapt to our feet. Sherlock and Watson started barking hysterically.

"What happened?" Jillian cried. "Why are people screaming?"

Vance stiffened with alarm, whipped the binoculars back out, and stared hard at the ravine. He stifled a curse and immediately pulled his two girls in tight against his chest.

"No, don't look," I heard him tell Victoria, as she started to protest.

Jillian clutched my arm and tears formed in her eyes. She was frantically gesturing at the jumping platform. Not wanting her to say anything out loud, which could frighten Vance's kids, I looked for myself to see what the problem was, only I had a nagging feeling I knew what I was going to find.

The bungee cord twisted and turned as it bounced up and down in the ravine. The problem was, there was no jumper attached to it. C2 was no longer there!

SEVEN

"How is he?" I asked, as soon as Jillian and I entered the hospital and the two of us saw Vance reading a magazine in the waiting room. Pacing nearby was the leader of the seemingly accident-prone Daredevils, Thor. One look at the Daredevils' leader confirmed that he had taken the latest accident very badly. Then again, I can only assume he's been having one hellaciously crappy month so far.

"He's gonna pull through," Vance assured us. "Don't get me wrong, he's not out of the woods yet, but the doctors do expect him to make a full recovery."

"Finish the story," Thor miserably said, as he passed Vance during his fervent pacing.

"There's more?" Jillian hesitantly asked.

Vance nodded. "C2 will recover, but he's got a long road ahead of him. Both of his legs are broken. He's got fractured ribs, a dislocated shoulder, and a concussion. Hey, where are the dogs? You didn't leave them outside, did you? It's too warm for them to be left in the car today."

"You sound like Harry," I mock-accused. "No worries. We dropped them off at the house before coming here. That's why we were late."

"Ah."

"How did this happen?" I asked, as Jillian and I took chairs next to Vance. "I mean, I would think that checking the bungee rope for cracks and breaks should be high on the Check Before Jumping list all platform operators should adhere to."

"It wasn't the rope," Thor said, as he passed for the third time. "It was the harness."

"C2's harness broke?" I repeated, dumbfounded. "I don't think I've ever heard of a harness breaking during a jump. The rope, sure, but the harness? Not once."

"Ditto," Thor agreed. "Leave it to us to have the first."

A thought occurred, and I had to ask.

"Natural causes?"

This brought Thor to a stop. "Huh?"

"The harness," I clarified. "Did it break due to natural causes?"

"How do you have natural causes for a nylon harness?" Thor wanted to know.

I shrugged. "I don't know. Repeated use?"

"Then the harness should have been replaced," Jillian softly added. "I had a friend who was an avid bungee jumper. He said they maintain strict reports and records on the ropes, including frequent inspections to see if any signs of wear can be seen. If so, then the rope is replaced. The same goes for the harness."

"Someone tampered with it," Vance guessed.

Thor sighed and sank down into the closest chair. "It'd have to be. That's the only thing I can figure. Someone tampered with C2's harness, and I don't know why."

Vance's notebook appeared. "Has anyone looked at that harness yet? I mean, do we know which part broke?"

Thor practically leapt out of his chair and resumed his pacing. He tapped his chest. "Right here, right where the carabiner connects the shoulder straps with the lower part of the harness. The EMTs had to cut it off of him, but I could still see that the strap holding the ring in place, where the carabiner attaches to the harness, had been ripped away."

"Wouldn't it take a lot of force to rip something like that?" Vance wanted to know.

Thor nodded. "Minimum breaking strength for those harnesses is typically 6,000 lbs."

"There's no way that thing broke on its own," I whispered.

"My thoughts exactly," Thor agreed. "His harness had to have been tampered with. I just don't know why."

"Or how," Vance added.

"How well did he get along with the other Daredevils?" I asked.

Thor shrugged. "As well as to be expected. I mean, he pretty much kept to himself. I don't ever remember him mentioning he had any friends outside of our club. But damn, was he good on a computer. Any time any of us had an electronic issue, be it with computer, tablet, or phone, C2 was our guy. Hell, I've seen him take a phone that had been put through a wash cycle and somehow revive it."

"Where was he last year?" I grumped, thinking back to the time I hadn't remembered my phone was in my pants pocket until the rinse cycle.

"You told me you lost that phone," Jillian said, as she turned to me.

"Yep. Lost it, as in, lost it to stupidity. It means the same thing in my book."

Jillian giggled, but not before shaking her head in exasperation.

"No friends, and no family here in town," I mused. "Sounds like he's someone who pretty much kept indoors and preferred it that way."

Thor nodded. "Exactly."

"He doesn't strike me as the type of guy who would associate with your Daredevils," Vance decided as he frowned. "What made him join up? Did he ever say?"

Thor shook his head. "No, it's not an admission requirement. If you want to join, and have some fun with new friends, then we're the club for you. At least, we were."

I looked helplessly at Vance. I really didn't have any comforting words of wisdom to pass along, especially when looking at the Daredevils' past run of bad luck. Two deaths and one almost-death? It didn't look good for this group of thrill-seekers.

"What are you going to do?" Vance asked.

"I don't think I have a choice," Thor responded. "I don't want anyone else to get hurt. Seeing how someone is trying to sabotage me, I'm gonna have to close the club. I just wish if it is me they want, then just come after me and get it over with. Leave my team alone."

"You'd better not be thinking about grounding the 'Devils," a new voice said.

We turned to see the rest of the Daredevils walk through the hospital's main entrance and stop in front of their leader. Curious to see how this was going to play out, Vance, Jillian, and I carefully stepped off to the side.

As the Daredevils argued and pleaded with their leader to keep their club open, I caught sight of someone peeking inside the hospital from the parking lot outside. It was Ash. Angry and ticked that the marshal still refused to be seen in public, I gave Jillian's hand a squeeze, and then pulled it free from hers. Curious as to where I was going, she followed, as did Vance.

"There you are," I angrily accused, as soon as the sliding front entry doors hissed closed behind me. "Dude, I don't know what evidence you have, or if you've made any deductions yet, but this has got to stop."

"I couldn't agree more," Vance added. "Listen, Marshal, Zack and I have only been on two excursions since joining this group, and look at what has happened! One death and one seriously injured. Zack is right. If you have enough to make an arrest, then I'd suggest you do it now. You do, don't you?"

I watched Ash's face fall and I knew precisely how much the good marshal had: zilch.

"You don't have a clue who Jerod is, do you?" I guessed.

Ash reluctantly shook his head. "I just need some more time, fellas."

"More t-time?" Jillian stuttered. "More time?? Are you kidding? Look at what's happened, Marshal Binson! One person falls off a raft and drowns, and a second nearly plummets to his death! I'm with Zachary and Vance on this. You're not putting my fiancé, and my good friend, into any more needless danger, do you hear me?"

"Do you, or do you not, have any type of case built up yet?" Vance wanted to know.

Ash sadly shook his head. "I don't."

"You've been here for how long now?" I wanted to know.

"Almost a month," Ash admitted.

"On the taxpayer's dime?" I demanded. "Tell me that's not the case."

A blue-suited janitor appeared just then, pushing a neon-yellow mop bucket out the front entrance. He promptly headed for the parking lot. My guess would be he was planning on dumping the water outside.

"It isn't the case," Ash admitted, after glancing

at the passing janitor. "I was given two weeks. After that, my expenses here would be covered on my own dime. So, I had to find some cheaper accommodations if I wanted to stay, which I did. I'm actually renting a lady's spare bedroom right now. Much more economical."

"And your bosses are okay with you spending so much time trying to apprehend the same guy?" Vance skeptically asked.

Ash nodded. "Of course. I wouldn't be here if they weren't. Listen, just bear with me for a few more days, okay? I know I can figure out which identity Jerod is hiding behind. Listen, I have to go. I have a sneaky feeling Jerod knows what I look like, so I don't want to be seen talking to you two, okay? I'll be in touch."

Much to my surprise, I watched the marshal hurry over to an older blue Corvette, fire it up, and then peel out of the parking lot.

"Do federal marshals typically drive around in classic sports cars?" Jillian asked.

I shook my head. "I wouldn't think so. It is a nice-looking car."

"It's a 1967 Corvette Stingray," Jillian confidently told me. "Coupe."

I turned to my fiancée with surprise written all over my face.

"I remember seeing one that looked like that when I was in high school," Jillian explained. "I thought it was just as pretty then as I do now. My father noticed my interest in Corvettes, so he bought me this poster of nothing but Corvettes, one for each year they had been in production. I became quite adept at guessing a 'Vette's age just by looking at it."

Shrugging, I grinned at Jillian and then frowned as I hooked a thumb in the direction Ash had gone.

"So, what's the general consensus of our pal, Ash?"

Jillian eyed me, turned to look back at the direction Ash had gone, then back at me. She tenderly took my hands in hers, looked me straight in the eyes, and shook her head.

"I think he's full of crap."

My eyebrows shot up. "Not what I was expecting you to say."

"Oh, trust me, I have a completely different word in mind," my fiancée told me. "I don't buy his story that he's determined Jerod's false identity. He's just as clueless as we are. I'm convinced he told us that just to placate us."

Vance nodded. "Agreed."

"What should we do now?" I inquired. I pointed back inside the hospital. "Should we go back in there?"

Jillian nodded. "I would. I'd like to hear for myself that … C2, is it? I'd like to know C2 is going to be okay."

Hand-in-hand, Jillian and I walked back inside, with Vance trailing behind us. However, we walked ourselves right into a full-blown argument. From the sounds of things, half the Daredevils were wanting to ... no, I'd better make that *demanding* the club be shut down until this run of bad luck had run its course. The other half steadfastly supported keeping the club open, for obvious reasons. Each side, it would seem, was trying to convince the other. How? By continually raising their voices so they could shout over the others.

Bad luck? Is that what the rest of the Daredevils think this is? Clearly, their fearless leader has refrained from sharing his suspicions with the rest of the group. Then there were those opposed to disbanding the group, spearheaded by Yeti. Thor's second-in-command was pushing to keep the club open, in honor and memory of Hades and Jitters. I then heard talk inquiring how C2 was holding up, and that was all it took to start the argument all over again.

It was giving me a headache. I felt Jillian tug my hand.

"Let's go where it's quieter. I can see some chairs over there."

Once the three of us were comfortably sitting —in silence, mind you—where we would be in a position to hear if someone had an update on C2, I pulled out my phone and started looking through the various pictures I had taken. Jillian slipped her left arm through my right and leaned up against me so she could watch what I was doing. It took me a few minutes to find the correct starting point, but once I did, I couldn't help but laugh.

Before I describe the first picture, I feel I should point out my current routine whenever the dogs and I are on a case and they express interest in something, seemingly insignificant or otherwise. Since I know full well that—somehow—there'll be something in the picture which will be pertinent to the case, I've taken to simply pointing my phone in the general direction the dogs were barking (in case I was driving) and taking at least four to five pictures at a time. When you're trying to drive and hold a phone at the same time, all without allowing your eyes to leave the road, then you really don't have a clue what is getting its picture taken. My phone, when the camera is enabled, will allow me to press any available button (except the power button) to take the shot.

Remember that.

Now then, the first picture was taken when Vance and I were having lunch at Casa de Joe's. It was the day we met Marshal Ash Binson. If memory served, a guy walked by our table and both dogs started woofing. Actually, I believe Sherlock had even given one of his low howls of frustration. Why? I didn't know. To shut him up, I took a few pictures. What had I managed to capture?

I stared at the screen with an embarrassed smile on my face. The person who had walked by was a guy in his mid-fifties, wearing a black shirt and camouflage pants. None of my shots had a picture of the guy's face. What I ended up taking a picture of was the guy's backside. There it was, centered on my screen for everyone to see.

Jillian started laughing, as did Vance.

"Not one of my best pictures, I will admit," I hastily said.

However, the next three pictures were all of the same guy, showing him in mid-step as he walked away from us. Yes, his rear was prevalent in every photograph.

"Well, that's not awkward at all," I chuckled, as I hurriedly swiped the display, eager to get to the next picture.

The next set of photos were of my attempt to take a picture of Gary's Grocery, all while driving in reverse, mind you. Sherlock had started his low woofing the moment I had returned to my Jeep after buying a few things from the store. I stared at my attempts and had to laugh.

Picture #1 was of the open sky, with no buildings visible. Picture #2 had a corner of the grocery store visible, but it was super blurry. The third photo managed to get the grocery store's sign in focus, and the fourth was of the pickup truck I almost rear-ended when I wasn't paying attention to my driving.

"Why did you take a picture of this truck?" Vance wanted to know, as he studied my phone's display.

"It's evidence," I stated matter-of-factly.

Vance looked up. "Of what?"

"That I shouldn't drive and tinker with my phone at the same time."

"You told me you were going to cut down on that," Jillian scolded.

"It's only because Sherlock was barking at something in that direction."

Vance looked at the other three photos. "Well, the first two are pretty much useless. The third is of Gary's Grocery's sign, but I don't know how that helps us."

"Neither do I," I admitted.

"What's next?" Vance eagerly asked.

I took my phone back from Vance and swiped right. There was a decent shot of Rupert's Gas & Auto.

"Gas station," I reported.

Vance scribbled some notes in his notebook.

"Which dog barked this time?" my detective friend asked.

I stared at Vance as though he had just spoken in Russian. "Which dog? What difference does it make?"

"Just a theory," Vance told me. "Do you remember which one?"

I sat back in my chair and thought about that day. "Let's see. I was headed east, back into town. The gas station was on my left. Watson likes to sit directly behind me, with Sherlock on the right side. I remember whoever started barking first was doing so right behind me, so the answer would be Watson."

"Your dogs have their own seats in your Jeep?" Vance chuckled. "Okey dokey."

"We figure it's because Sherlock likes to keep Zachary in his sight at all times," Jillian explained.

Vance shrugged. "All right. That I'll buy."

I flipped through the other four pictures I took. Of the five, four were decent, and one was blurry. All the usable shots showed only one thing, as far as I could tell: they were simply shots of the gas station. I didn't see any strange cars or people milling about. In fact, the station was rather quiet. We had been the only customer in the store at that time of the day.

"This can't be this difficult," Vance grumbled.

"What's difficult?" Jillian wanted to know.

Frustrated, Vance pointed at my phone.

"That. We're grown adults. We're educated, intelligent. Yet, why can't we figure out what the dogs are looking at here?"

I stifled a chuckle. "Maybe that's because there's nothing happening in any of these?"

"Whenever we're working a case, how often does that happen?" Vance muttered. "Take that time Sherlock found the syringe full of peanut oil."

"The same syringe you ended up jabbing into your finger?" I recalled.

Vance's face colored. "Yeah, that'd be the one. Not only did he find the syringe, he also zeroed in on the muffin cups, too."

"And they brought our attention to the salal berry bushes," Jillian added. "That was the same case."

Vance snapped his fingers. "That's right. I forgot about that. My point is, whatever catches their attention is relevant in some fashion. You've been taking pictures of everything they bark at, which is brilliant, by the way. However, why can't we figure out how it's pertinent to the case?"

"I don't see how a gas station could be relevant," I decided, as I flipped back and forth between the photos.

As I reviewed the pictures, I inadvertently swiped right, when I meant to swipe left. A new photo appeared, and this was from earlier in the day.

I was staring at the jump point on the bridge. Wordlessly, I showed the photo to Jillian and Vance. The two of them fell silent as they studied the tiny picture.

"I remember this one," Vance stated. "I mean, I should. I was there. Sherlock started it, didn't he?"

"Yep." I nodded.

"Do you think he knew the harness was going to break?" Jillian softly asked.

"I have no idea," I admitted, and tapped the phone's display. "I kinda got the impression that he was looking at someone beside C2."

That got Vance's attention. "Oh? Who?"

I zoomed in on the picture as much as I was able. "I don't know. I didn't see anyone who stood out."

"Can I see that?"

The phone was passed to Vance.

"Hmm. Look here. Do you see this guy?"

Jillian and I leaned close.

"What about him?" I asked.

Vance tapped the screen again, "I think this might be the same guy from earlier, Zack. From the restaurant, I mean."

I finally noticed what Vance was pointing at and took the phone back. I hate to admit, I had to hold the thing up close to my face.

"I'm getting you an eye exam," Jillian stated.

"Psssht. It's nothing to worry about. Vance, is this the guy you're talking about? Him? Just because he's wearing camouflage pants? You have no idea if that's the same person. He's too far away."

"Based on Sherlock's behavior, it could be," Vance protested.

Jillian took my phone and studied the image for herself. She looked over at Vance and waggled the phone.

"You think this person is the same person in Zachary's butt shot?"

"He was walking away from me," I argued. "Of course I was gonna get a shot of his butt."

"All I'm saying is it's a possibility."

"What about this one, Zachary?" Jillian asked, having swiped left to review the previous pictures.

I leaned over Jillian's shoulder to see what she was looking at.

"Oh, that. I wouldn't worry about that."

"What is it?" Vance asked, curious.

"It's a picture of A Lazy Afternoon."

Vance's eyebrows shot up. "The bookstore? Zack, isn't that Clara Hanson's shop?"

I felt my face flush red. Man alive, did that woman creep me out. Clara was a woman in her mid-seventies, but acted like she was decades younger. The problem was, she dressed like she was still a teenager. There are some things you simply can't unsee. The icing on the cake was Clara's inability to not invade your personal space. She ignored personal boundaries and preferred to get right up in your face.

So ... whenever I saw her coming, I usually made sure I was going in the opposite direction.

"I knew it!" Vance triumphantly exclaimed. "I knew you liked her, buddy! Good for you!"

A giggle escaped from Jillian's lips. My eyes narrowed as I studied my fiancée's lovely face, only she was unable to look at me without laughing. I looked over at Vance and contemplated flipping him the bird, but somehow—and I don't know how—Jillian chose that moment to take my hand in hers and gently, but firmly, dig her nails in.

"The dogs barked at her place as soon as I drove by," I complained. "I didn't want to take a picture but felt I didn't have a choice."

"It's a great shot," Vance admitted, as he studied the photo. "What, did you pull over and stop?"

"It was a red light, and you can bite me."

Vance chuckled as he looked down at his notes. "Man in camouflage pants, grocery store, gas station, trash can in a picnic area, another guy in camouflage, and Clara's bookstore. I gotta admit, I have no idea how it all fits together."

"I think I know what this means," I said, as I lowered my voice.

Vance and Jillian automatically inched closer.

"What?" Vance eagerly asked.

"It means that dogs are clearly smarter than humans."

Vance snorted, while Jillian giggled. I was in the process of sliding my phone back into my pocket when it started ringing. I glanced at the display and saw an unknown number.

"Unknown," I reported. "Should I take it?"

Vance shrugged. "It's up to you. I don't think it'll hurt anything. Get many crank calls?"

I shook my head. "No. At least, not until Abigail Lawson gets ahold of my cell number."

Abigail Lawson was a distant relative of my late wife's. She's the one who thought I shouldn't have been awarded ownership of my winery, Lentari Cellars, and was doing her damnedest to wrest control away from me. Seeing how I haven't heard from her for so long, I could only groan and cross my fingers that this wasn't her.

"Hello?"

"Zack? It's Ash."

"Hey, Marshal. What's up? What number are you calling from?"

"I'm calling from the place I'm staying. Listen, I need to ask a huge favor."

"We've already granted you a huge favor, Ash. We joined those damn Daredevils, didn't we?"

"Yes, you did, and I have no right to ask another favor. However, I'm forced to."

"What do you want?" I hesitantly asked.

"I need you two to stick with the Dysfunctional Daredevils. We must bring Jerod to justice."

"You're assuming that the Daredevils will still be around. Wait, are they? Do you know something that we don't?"

"It was just announced on social media that not only are the Daredevils still together, they've agreed on their next excursion."

"Isn't that a little premature?" I asked, dumbfounded.

"What's the matter?" Vance whispered.

"Ash, I'm putting you on speakerphone. Vance is here, and so is Jillian."

"Oookkkaayy..." Ash slowly said, as though the addition of more ears was a bad thing.

"Say that again, would you? What you just told me. Repeat that, please."

"I was saying that the group has already organized their next excursion."

"How is that even possible?" Vance demanded. "Thor was preparing to disband the group at the hospital. Hell, we're still at the hospital, and we haven't heard anything yet."

Right about then, we noticed that there was no noise coming from the main lobby. As a matter of fact, none of us had noticed when the heated arguments and conversations had died off. Vance quickly got to his feet and hurried through the open doorway, intent on seeing for himself what the status was.

"What's going on?"

"Vance just left this little side room we've been sitting in and is attempting to verify what you've just told us. Uh, oh. He's coming back, and it looks like Thor is with him. You'd better get going."

"Roger that. Zack? Please. Stick with the group. I'm asking for your help, as a friend."

"We'll see. That's the only thing I can give you at the moment."

"Then it'll have to do. Bye."

The phone call ended just as Vance returned, followed closely by Thor.

"There you are," the chairman of the Dare-devils exclaimed. "I thought you had gone home. Listen, good news! Our next trip is planned!"

"You can't be serious," Jillian scoffed. She was frowning and her arms were folded across her chest.

"Look, let's be honest," Thor began. "Chances are, the 'Devils are done. You know that. I know that. However, before we're officially disbanded, or else I'm arrested, we're going to go on one last trip."

I took a deep breath and eyed the group's chairman. "No disrespect intended, but, umm, there have been two accidents, and fatalities were involved."

"C2 will pull through," Thor proudly stated. "So that's one fatality."

Vance held up a hand, with two fingers extended. "There's two, buddy. Don't forget about Hades. And, if it wasn't for some blind luck, C2 would be number three."

Thor's smile slowly melted off his face. He sighed heavily and sat down on my left.

"Look, if we don't do something now, and I mean in the next day or so, then we'll lose that chance forever. I, for one, would like to think that Hades and Jitter's deaths weren't in vain. So, the day after tomorrow, provided we haven't been shut down, we're giving the Dysfunctional Daredevils an appropriate send-off. One final thrill, if you will."

"And that would be…?" I nervously asked.

"I don't want to know what you've come up with," Jillian whispered. She was still frowning at the head of the Daredevils.

"I can't speak for you two, but I'm fairly certain I'm not gonna like this, am I?" Vance groaned.

Thor's face lit up with a smile. "My friends, if this is our time, then let's go out with a bang. Hopefully, not literally. We're going on my favorite type of adventure: skydiving!"

EIGHT

Something just doesn't add up," I was say-ing, on the following day. Jillian and I, along with the dogs, were out for a drive on the open highway. The weather was cooperating, the dogs were happily spraying doggie drool all over the sides of my classic 1930 Ruxton Sedan, and do you know what? I couldn't be happier.

For those that may or may not remember, this was the car that was previously owned by Dame Hilda Highland. Unbeknownst to us, when Jillian purchased the Highland House as an investment last year, the classic roadster came along with it. Seeing how I drooled over the thing every time I saw a picture of it, Jillian very generously gave the car to me.

Not particularly caring for the standard gray tone paint that had been on the car, and wanting to restore the glory a car like that deserved, we had it repainted. Dark forest green, if you must know. Jillian's choice.

The garage that had been tasked with caring for the car over the years had done a remarkable job, which is why I extended the contract and have them service the car on a monthly basis. As it turned out, it had only taken less than ten grand to make the car road worthy. Well, if you want to get technical, it was already road worthy, only I needed to add a few changes to the car. That meant new paint job, new stereo, new tires, and newly upholstered seats.

Trust me, this thing purrs like a kitten. Every time I brought this lovely old gal out for a drive, people would stop me and offer to purchase the car outright, for sums of money that would make you dizzy. A polite—but firm—thanks-but-no-thanks always ensued, no matter how much the price was raised. Some things just weren't for sale. And I, being the sentimental fool that I was, was not about to part with a car that had so much history behind it.

On this particular occasion, the two of us had decided we needed a break. We needed some quiet time where we didn't have to think about work, writing, or the impending doom that was waiting for me just around the corner. Skydiving. Are you kidding me? Isn't that what poor Hades had been doing when he had lost his life? Something about a parachute not opening properly?

A soft hand was suddenly placed over mine. I looked over at my fiancée and saw that she was studying me intently.

"If it makes you feel any better," Jillian began, "I'm not happy about this, either. I do hope you're planning on calling this thing off, Zachary. I don't want you risking your life by jumping out of a plane."

"I have absolutely no intention of it," I assured her. "I was just recalling how poor Hades lost his life. Skydiving accident, and I think Vance said that a couple of hikers found a piece of him."

Jillian frowned and shook her head. "That's an unpleasant picture."

"Yeah, I'm sorry about that. I shouldn't have said anything. It's just that …"

"What?" Jillian asked, after noticing I had trailed off.

"I'm starting to have some serious doubts about our friend, the marshal."

"Doubts as to his ability to apprehend this fugitive?" Jillian asked.

"Honestly? I think I have doubts about everything. I'm even starting to wonder if *he* might be this Jerod person we're looking for."

"U.S. Marshal Binson is not a killer," Jillian matter-of-factly stated.

"How do you know?" I challenged. "Shave off that beard and he could pass for someone in his mid-twenties. He has the right build. And besides, he's the right height."

We both fell silent as we mulled over the similarities between what we knew of the suspect, and what we knew of the marshal. Jillian had stopped outright defending him, which spooked me more than anything else she could have done. I suspected she was having second thoughts now, too. How, then, could we prove that the marshal was either a legitimate lawman, or else a serial killer in disguise?

Sherlock jumped over to right side of the car and thrust his nose out of the window. He woofed. Moments later, Watson joined him. Before I knew it, both of the warning woofs morphed into frenzied barking.

I started reaching for my phone the moment both dogs had arrived at the window. Jillian saw me fumbling for my phone and, instead, pulled her own out. She looked at me and questioningly waggled her phone.

"If you'll tell me what you want a picture of, then I'll be more than happy to take it. That way, you can keep both hands on the wheel."

"Thanks. I appreciate it. So, tell me, what's on that side of the car?" Traffic was picking up and I was really glad I didn't have to take my eyes off the road. I trusted my own driving, sure, but it was the other guy I was concerned about.

"Well, we're coming up on 3rd Street," Jillian informed me. She glanced out the right side of the car and shook her head. "I really don't see what could be ... huh."

"Huh?" I repeated, confused. "You see something, don't you? What is it?"

In response, Jillian raised her phone up to her face and snapped several pictures.

"Well, I think you might want to make a left on

3rd."

"I do? Why?"

"Zachary, there's a certain blue Corvette parked on the side of the street over there that might interest you."

Thankful—for once—that the traffic light had turned red, and we were already stopped, I glanced over and felt my eyebrows threaten to jump off my face. Jillian was right. There was the aforementioned sports car. Wasn't that the one Ash had been driving? What was he doing here, running an errand?

Acknowledging my curiosity had been piqued, I pulled up behind the shiny blue 'Vette and parked. I glanced over at Jillian, intent on telling her to wait in the car with the dogs, when I caught sight of the store Ash had parked in front of: A Lazy Afternoon. It was Clara Hanson's shop, and damned if I couldn't stop myself shuddering. How badly did I want to find out what Ash has been up to?

I was in the process of pulling my seat belt back across my lap when I heard the tell-tale click of the passenger seat belt being disengaged. Jillian had opened the door, stepped out, and was reaching inside for the dogs' leashes when she noticed I hadn't budged.

"What are you doing? Don't you want to go inside to see what your marshal is doing in a bookstore?"

I made a point of glancing at the shop's front

door, then up at the wooden shop sign, and then back at the steering wheel, all without saying anything.

"She's not that bad, Zachary. Come on. We're going inside."

Jillian and the dogs disappeared through the door just as I stepped out of the car, muttering like Yosemite Sam.

"Freakin' give-me-the-willies creepy ol' lady," I muttered under my breath.

Stepping into the small bookstore, several things became apparent right off the bat. First, Ash was nowhere to be seen. Second, my desire to get out of this store without being noticed by the proprietor was not gonna happen.

"Zack! It's so good of you to come visit me, darlin'! Just a second. I'll be right there, Sugar."

While I cringed and waited for the inevitable invasion of my personal space to happen, I became aware of another presence. Before I could turn to see what it was, I heard a rapid fluttering of wings, and just like that, I had the store's alarm system perched on my shoulder. An African gray parrot, by the name of Ruby, nuzzled up against my face and softly cooed. I reached up to stroke the bird's head when the soft gray fluffball surprised me again by leaping into my open hand. Right on cue, Sherlock fired off a couple of warning woofs.

"Heavens above, I don't know what's gotten into that bird," Clara was saying, as she navigated her way through the narrow aisles of books. She placed herself in front of me with her hands on her hips and stared, amazed, at her parrot. Unfortunately, I could only stare at her, with my mouth open.

"Like what you see, darlin'?"

My mouth snapped closed. Hoo boy. You'll have to give me a moment so as to better describe the scene before me.

Clara's hair, which is usually styled in the manner of Marge Simpson's, was now cotton candy pink and just about as fluffy. It was arranged in a bright, poufy afro, and looked as ridiculous as any of the other myriad of styles she has tried. Moving past the hair, I have to take a moment to mention the outfit. Ms. Clara Hanson, septuagenarian, had on a skin-tight leopard print bodysuit. I learned that day there were things that I simply couldn't unsee, no matter how much I tried. Or willed. Completing the ghastly look was a pair of fur-lined black ankle boots.

Horrified, I glanced over at my fiancée. Jillian, much to her credit, confided to me later that she had nearly gasped out loud when she saw the overall look. We both agreed that Ms. Hanson's fashion sense, while never that tasteful to begin with, was definitely waning. I truly believed that the next stop on Clara Hanson's whack-job senility train was a little town called Insanity, and it was located just around the corner.

"Ruby, what are you doing? Get back on your perch, you silly thing."

"Give us a kiss, Precious! Give us a kiss!"

The shop owner waggled a finger at the bird. "If Zack kisses anyone, it'll be me."

"The only one I'll be kissing is standing right over there," I pointed out, as I tried valiantly to suppress my desire to do one of those full-body twitches. "I'm sure you've met her before, haven't you?"

Taken aback, Clara turned to see where I was pointing. To her credit, she acted as though she hadn't seen Jillian or the dogs enter.

"Jillian! How are you, dearie? I didn't see you there. Zachary, don't be silly. Of course I know her. Wait a moment. Are you trying to tell me the two of you are an item?"

"Oh, you and your memory," Jillian teased. "You know full well that Zachary and I are engaged. I told you the last time you were in Cookbook Nook, remember?"

Clara rubbed her chin and tried to look thoughtful.

"I don't seem to recall, dearie. But, it doesn't really matter now, does it? I'm so happy for you two!"

I shared a look with Jillian. Clara certainly didn't sound like she was happy, nor did she look it. Maybe now she'll start respecting my personal space?

"Let me just get her off your shoulder, Zackie-Boy."

Zackie-Boy? Where the hell did that come from?

Clara then proceeded to practically throw her arms around me, while rubbing up against my chest, in an *attempt* to reclaim her parrot. Unfortunately, that meant her front was now rubbing on my front, and if I wasn't thoroughly grossed out before, I sure as hell was now. Ruby, properly spooked, flew off my shoulder and landed back on her perch, near the cashier's station. A few moments later, the small parrot was squawking her displeasure.

"I'm squealin' from the feelin', Precious! Squealin' from the feelin'!"

Jillian's shocked look mirrored my own. The only way Ruby could have picked up that particular phrase was if Clara had repeated it over and over. One look at the proprietor confirmed it. Thankfully, at least Clara appeared to be embarrassed.

"What did I tell you about repeating that, Ruby? It's not funny anymore!"

Ruby cackled with delight and bobbed her head a few times.

"Clara," Jillian interjected, "can I ask you about something?"

"You bet your hot young man you can," Clara chortled. "What can I do for you, dearie?"

Jillian pointed outside. "Can you tell us if you saw the person who parked that Corvette outside?"

Surprised, Clara looked outside and walked over to the front windows. She pointed at the blue sports car as if to verify she didn't believe we were talking about the same car.

"That one? The Stingray? Well, of course I saw who drove it."

"Where did he go?" I eagerly asked.

"He?" Clara repeated, as she frowned. "There's no *he* involved. I drove that car, Zackie-Boy."

I let the shudder-worthy moniker slide for now.

"You? Why would you be driving that car?"

"Because it's mine, dearie! My Prius is in the shop. I was forced to drive that beast."

"There must be more than one in town," I decided. I glanced down at the dogs, but was surprised to see both of them staring straight at Clara. Typically, neither dog would give the crackpot senior the time of day. That nagging voice inside my head was telling me that I needed to probe a little further. "So, um, have you loaned that car out to anyone lately?"

"My Prius? Absolutely not. No one drives my baby but me."

"I'm talking about the 'Vette," I kindly pointed out.

"That car was my late husband's pride and joy," Clara wistfully recalled. "I've never really known why he enjoyed it so much. It may look pretty, but oh honey, does it ever drive rough. Wait. Are you wanting to know if I've loaned out my Corvette to anyone? You're talking about my late husband's car, aren't you?"

"We know you probably haven't," Jillian soothed. "We're sorry to bother you. We'll head out now."

"No one has driven that car but me for years," Clara continued, completely ignoring Jillian's attempt to take our leave. "No one but that nice Mr. Binson, that is."

Both corgis woofed. Jillian and I froze, mid-step, on our way out the door. As one, we turned back to the shopkeeper.

"Come again?" I said.

"He's such a nice-looking young man that I offered to let him use the car while he was staying with me."

"Ash Binson … is staying … with you?" I incredulously repeated.

Clara happily nodded. "It's so nice to have a man in the house again."

"Why is he staying in your house?" Jillian politely, but firmly, asked.

"He's renting a room from me, of course," Clara proudly exclaimed. "He's the one who's overseeing the oil change being performed on my car right now. As soon as it's finished, he'll be stopping by here to exchange cars. I'll be glad to get my car back. I … is that the roadster I've heard so much about? Parked next to my blue beast?"

I nodded. As God is my witness, I have no idea why I was prompted to say the following. "If you like smooth rides, then you'd love a ride in the Ruxton. They did a great job with that car."

"Oooo, I accept!" Clara happily cried.

I blinked a few times. "Wait, what?"

"I'd love to go on a ride with you in that wonderful car of yours."

Oh, snap. I looked at my fiancée, hopeful that she'd come to my aid. But did she?

"I think you're free this Friday night, Zachary," Jillian said, as she made a point of looking at her phone's calendar app. "You could show her a good time then."

My eyes narrowed. There was no way in hell that I was gonna allow myself to be alone, in a car, with Clara Hanson. Ever.

"Perhaps another time," I hastily said, suppressing what had to be my third or fourth shudder since stepping foot inside this blasted store. "Thank you very much for your help. The dogs are getting restless, so we'd best be going."

"Don't be a stranger, sweetie," Clara cooed. She looked over at Jillian and her smile thinned. "See you around, dearie!"

"I can't believe you invited her for a drive in your car," Jillian laughed, the moment we pulled away. "And here, all this time, I thought you didn't like her."

"I *don't* like her," I clarified. "At all. She has creeped me out from day one. *Blech.*"

My phone rang. Wanting to keep the car as original as possible, I had opted for a standard, classic in-dash radio. That meant no Bluetooth, which meant I could be ticketed and fined by the state of Oregon if I answered while behind the wheel. Thankfully, I had a passenger.

"It's Vance," Jillian reported, as she looked at the display. She tapped the screen a few times and then sat back in her seat.

"Hello, Vance, it's Jillian. You have us both. Zachary is driving, so I won't let him anywhere near the phone."

"Good for you. I was calling to give you an update."

"That's good timing," Jillian returned. "We have one for you, too."

"Oh? You do? What's your news about?"

"It's about Marshal Binson," Jillian answered.

I nodded. "Yeah. Do you remember that Corvette we saw him driving?"

"The blue coupe? Yeah, what about it?"

"Well, it belongs to Clara Hanson."

"You're kidding."

"Wish I was, buddy. And it gets better."

"I'm listening."

"He's renting a room from her," Jillian said.

"Ash is renting a room from Clara Hanson? There's a mental picture I didn't need."

"Right?"

"Why the hell would he want to rent a room from her?"

"Proof positive he's not from around here," I quipped.

"What did you find out, Vance?" Jillian asked.

"Oh, only our friend Mr. Binson is thiiiiiis close

to being kicked out of the U.S. Marshal Service."

My eyes widened with surprise. I glanced over at Jillian, but something on her face told me this didn't surprise her that much.

"You knew, didn't you?" I mock-teased.

"Knew what?" Vance wanted to know.

"It looks like this doesn't come as a surprise to Jillian."

"The signs were there," my fiancée told me. "Unprofessional, haphazard investigative techniques, and willingness to put civilians in harm's way. I'm sorry to interrupt. What exactly did you find out, Vance?"

"Well, if you were wondering whether or not Ash Binson is legit, then rest assured, he is. But, if he's not careful, he won't be for much longer."

"What's that supposed to mean?" I wanted to know.

"Get this. Marshal Ash Binson is in deep shit with his bosses."

"Language," Jillian warned.

"Sorry. Umm, he's in deep crap. Looks like Ash Binson has been ordered to apprehend his suspect, or don't bother coming back."

I shared an incredulous look with Jillian.

"Really? That's a bit harsh. No wonder he's been out here so long."

"No wonder he's so desperate to keep you and Vance in this thrill-seeking club," Jillian surmised. "But, I wouldn't think the ability to apprehend a criminal would be contingent on whether or not the poor man can stay a marshal."

"Oh, it gets better. Apparently, what Marshal Binson neglected to tell us was that he was the one who lost Jerod in the first place."

I sat up straight in the Ruxton's driver seat.

"You mean ..."

"Ash was escorting the prisoner back to Texas when he lost him. Right from under his nose, according to the reports."

"He certainly left that part out earlier, didn't he?" I said, annoyed.

"From what I learned from the Texas Marshal Service office, they called Chief Nelson and said, and I quote, 'Leniency has expired. Return with the fugitive within the next three days or excursion will be terminated.' If it comes to that, then Ash Binson will be discharged from the marshal service."

"What do you suggest we do?" I asked, as I guided the smooth-rolling Ruxton onto the highway and gave it some gas.

"I say we tell Ash we have some new information and we should meet up for lunch. Or dinner."

"You should be the one to arrange that," Jillian told him. "You're the detective. You're the one with the influence to force his hand."

"I'll see what I can do. I'll call you back."

"He's the one who lost Jerod in the first place," I said. "That explains a lot."

"You shouldn't be so hard on him," Jillian told me. "Mistakes can happen to anyone."

"And because of his, several people have died."

"Do you really think Jerod is responsible for the disasters which have befallen the Daredevils?" Jillian asked.

I nodded. "I do. Either that, or Vance is gonna somehow blame me. It's only a matter of time before he starts calling me Grim Reaper."

My cell phone rang. Jillian answered, and put the call on speaker.

"That was quick. Is everything all right?"

"Yeah, it is, Jillian. Listen, Zack?"

"I'm here."

"We're set for dinner tonight."

"Who'll be there?" I wanted to know.

"You, me, and him."

I looked over at my fiancée and cringed. Jillian and I were due to have dinner together tonight. I really didn't want to mess that up. My hesitation must have told Vance all he needed to hear.

"I'm messing up your plans with Jillian, aren't I?"

"You are, buddy."

"I'm sorry. Listen, do this for me, and your next dinner out will be on the PVPD. Deal?"

"Anywhere I choose to go?" Jillian guardedly asked.

"Yes. Anywhere you'd like to go."

Ugh. That mean another night out at that fancy French restaurant that had the nasty frog legs I unknowingly ordered on my first visit. But, it was Jillian's favorite, so as long as she was amenable to changing our plans, who was I to argue?

"Yeah, okay. If Jillian's okay with it, then so am I."

"How much Crystal Rose do you think you can drink?" Jillian thoughtfully asked. "I could phone ahead and have them order an additional bottle or two."

I heard Vance groan. Crystal Rose was a type of champagne, a very expensive one at that. Jillian's favorite bottle of bubbly retails for $400 a pop, a fact not lost on my tightwad friend. I don't know. If I didn't have to pay for it, maybe I could choke down a glass or two?

"I'm sure I could put one away by myself," I said.

"Bull. I know you hate champagne, pal."

"Now's as good a time as any to give it another try, don't you think?"

"You're killing me, Zack."

"Which restaurant? Where are we meeting Ash?"

"Tre Formaggio."

"Oooo, they have fantastic breadsticks there," Jillian gushed. "Be sure to pick me up some."

"Deal," I grinned.

* * *

"So, what have you uncovered?" Ash asked, several hours later. He took a sip from his glass of ice water and looked expectantly at the detective. "What's so important that you wanted to meet now? Don't you have to get ready for your skydiving adventure tomorrow?"

Vance and I shared a look. We both knew damn well why the marshal had only ordered a glass of water, and not something more expensive, like a beer. He was obviously still here on his own dime and wanted to keep the expenses down as low as possible. What other possible explanation would exist for why someone would willingly stay with Clara Hanson?

"Well, a few new developments have come to light," Vance casually began.

Ash eagerly leaned forward. "Such as?"

"Like discovering why you have been hanging around Pomme Valley for so long."

Ash blinked a couple of times, confused. "I don't follow."

"How come you didn't tell us that you were the one responsible for allowing Jerod to escape?"

Ash's smile disappeared from his face. He slowly sat back in his chair and frowned.

"Who have you been talking to?"

"Just one Derrick Landcaster, back in Austin, Texas."

Ash groaned again.

"Do you know him?" I asked, even though I already knew the answer based on Ash's reaction.

"Yes. He's my boss. I don't understand why you felt it was necessary to call him."

"Because we had to know," I quietly answered.

Ash fixed me with a stare. "Know what?"

"If you were legit or possibly this Jerod character in disguise," Vance said.

A few moments passed before Ash finally responded.

"You doubted I was a marshal. That's just ... swell."

"We now know you are," Vance hesitantly began, "but, um ..."

"Oh, don't stop now," Ash scoffed. "By all means, finish the sentence."

"Your *leniency*, as your boss put it, has expired."

This must have been news to the marshal, because Ash was in the process of lifting his water glass, when he slowly lowered it back to the table.

"Expired?"

"Yeah. Looks like they're not too happy with how long it's taking you to apprehend your lost man."

Ash sighed and rubbed his temples.

"Why didn't you tell us?" I gently asked.

"Do you have any idea what a laughingstock I've been since Jerod managed to escape from under my very nose?" Ash sighed again and drained the rest of the water in his glass. "I thought if I could be the one to take him back into custody, then I'd be able to show my face back in Texas. I know full well I'm skating on thin ice with the Marshal Service right now. Why do you think I've been out in this tiresome town for so long? Oh. Sorry. No offense."

"None taken," Vance assured him. "My question for you is ... if what you say is true, then why did it take so long for you to notify my boss about your presence here? Why didn't you contact us the moment you arrived?"

"Because it would have made everything official," Ash miserably explained. "I'd have to disclose full details of why I was here. Your Chief Nelson has already been dropping some not-so-subtle hints that he wants a copy of all case files pertaining to Jerod Jones. I've managed to stall him so far ..."

"... no you haven't," Vance interrupted. "He started reaching out to the Marshal Service on the day we met. I can only imagine your bosses were covering for you, not wanting their dirty laundry known."

Ash groaned again and fixed the two of us with an imploring stare.

"You two are my last hope. We have one shot left at getting our hands on Jerod."

"And what's that?" I blindly asked.

It was Vance's turn to groan. "Don't you get it, Zack? He wants us to go sky diving."

"Yeah, about that," I slowly began, swallowing noisily as I did so, "I'm not thinking that it's gonna work out for me. I mean, come on. The Daredevils have already lost a member due to a skydiving accident. I really don't want to be the second."

"And if I told you that it wasn't an accident?" Ash asked, lowering his voice.

"It wouldn't surprise us that much," Vance decided. "I mean, let's face it. There's a known murderer rumored to be hiding out here, in Pomme Valley, and his only known acquaintance turns up dead? Am I the only one who isn't surprised by this?"

I raised my hand. "I'm not."

"Guys, I have a plan," Ash said, drawing skeptical looks from the two of us. "Just hear me out, okay?"

"The only thing I want to hear is that I won't be put in harm's way," I stubbornly declared. "I think my time with the Daredevils has come to an end."

"Ditto," Vance agreed.

"I hear you both. Now, listen. No one is going to be placed in harm's way. In fact, no one will be doing any skydiving whatsoever. We just have to make Jerod think we're going to, so he'll act on it, and therefore reveal himself."

"Act on it?" I incredulously repeated. "I don't know about you, buddy, but I most certainly don't want Jerod acting on anything."

"Let's hear what he has to say," Vance said. "Then, we can shoot him down, if necessary."

I waved a hand, indicating Ash had the floor.

"Okay, here's what we're going to do. First off, we're bringing in more people. They're going to all be officers."

I was already shaking my head. "That'll look too suspicious. You'll frighten Jerod off."

Ash nodded. "Without any type of explanation, that's true. However, a skydiving excursion is expensive. Most clubs get better rates if they can get more people involved."

Vance suddenly nodded. "I get it. You're going to pretend this other group of people is another skydiving club, is that it?"

Ash nodded. "Exactly. Since I know that Dean Babcock wants to ..."

"Who?" I interrupted.

"Dean Babcock," Ash repeated. "You know him as Thor."

"Ah. Sorry. Go on."

"Right. Thor wants to do another trip just as soon as possible, since he believes—rightfully so —that his adrenaline club is going to be closed down. Well, our cover story is that his team is hooking up with another team to help share the expenses."

"That means you'll have to let Thor in on your plan," Vance surmised. "You're going to have to hope that Thor and Jerod aren't pals and he doesn't warn him."

"I'm telling him nothing of the sort," Ash argued. "The marshals have already chartered the plane and announced it on social media. Sure enough, Thor's people took the bait. Our two teams have already hooked up."

"Surprising," I decided. "And impressive. Keep going, Ash."

"Right. Now, if any of the Daredevils wonder about the influx of new people, we can always say that skydiving excursions are the favorites of the adrenaline junkies, and as such, will usually attract more people. These jumping outfits will want to make as much as possible, so as long as the jumper meets their criteria, then there shouldn't be too many questions asked."

"How many people are you suggesting go with us?" I asked.

"Besides the Daredevils, there will be over a dozen undercover police officers on that plane including Vance."

Disheartened, I zeroed in on one word. "Plane? Are you actually suggesting we all go up, in the air?"

Ash nodded. "Well, yeah. We have to make it as believable as possible, don't we?"

"I'm not sure I'm liking this," I grumbled.

"What's your plan for getting Jerod to identify himself?" Vance wanted to know.

"That will fall on you," Ash told him.

"How long have you been working on this plan?" I wanted to know. "You seem to have it all thought out."

"A few days now. Don't interrupt. I'll lose my train of thought. Now, where was I?"

"You were going to tell me how Jerod is going to incriminate himself," Vance said.

"Ah. Right. That falls on you, detective."

"How?" Vance asked.

"You are going to make an announcement to the rest of the Daredevils that you now have a suspect in mind and expect him to be in custody in no time."

"And why would he believe me?" Vance asked, puzzled.

"Because, you and Zack are members of the group. You know they are suffering a horrific turn of bad luck. You just thought that a bit of good news would cheer them up."

"It's plausible," Vance decided.

"Have either of you been skydiving before?" Ash suddenly asked.

Both Vance and I shook our heads no.

"The outfit handling the jump will want to know, since you're beginners, if you want to do a tandem jump, which has a more experienced person attached behind you, or a static line jump, which essentially means your parachute is activated the instant you leave the plane."

"How about option C?" I asked, as I frowned at the marshal. "I choose not to jump at all."

"It's for appearance purposes only. You're a big guy, Zack, so I think you probably ought to opt for a static line jump. Vance, I think you could go either way."

"Hmmph," Vance snorted. One look at my friend confirmed he wasn't planning on jumping, either, regardless of the circumstances.

"When we're all up in the air," Ash continued, "we'll create some type of situation, which will abort the jump."

"What type of situation?" I wanted to know.

"Weather, mechanical, it really doesn't make a

difference," Ash explained.

Vance cleared his throat. "Just make a decision, and then let us know what that is before you do it, okay?"

Ash nodded. "Deal. Now, with cops everywhere on the plane, it'll just be a matter of time before Jerod panics and reveals himself."

"And if he doesn't?" I cautiously asked.

"Just look for the person who acts disappointed the jump is cancelled," Ash answered.

"But, that could be the entire Daredevil team," I protested. "How are we supposed to know which one is Jerod?"

"I think I know how I can answer that," Vance said. "Look, Zack. If the two of us start talking about the case on the way up, then …"

"… we paint one mother of a target on our backs," I interrupted.

"No, let me finish," Vance admonished. "If the specs of the case are out in the open, and we suggest we are very close to making an arrest, then what do you think Jerod is going to do if I let it slip, quietly to you, that there are a few undercover policemen on board?"

"He'll freak out and do something stupid," I guessed.

Ash nodded. "Exactly."

"This is not a good plan," I moaned.

"Look at it this way," Vance explained. "We won't be jumping out of any plane and we will be surrounded by cops. What could go wrong?"

I'm convinced I jinxed myself right then and there. Why? Less than twenty-four hours later, Vance and I would be free-falling, side by side, as we plummeted to the ground from thousands of feet up in the air.

NINE

"J ust what the ever lovin' hell am I doing here," Vance moaned, on the following day. "Maybe you and Tori are right: I am having a mid-life crisis. Why else would you find a grown man, with a great career and wonderful family, waiting inside a smelly airplane hangar with a bunch of kids..."

"... to jump out of a perfectly good airplane?" I finished for him. "Trust me, amigo. I've been having those same thoughts."

"I can't believe I let you two talk me into doing this," a third voice added.

Vance and I looked over at Harry, who looked as miserable as I have ever seen him. Both of us must have been giving our friend an unreadable look, because Harry immediately went on the defensive.

"What? Don't look at me like that. I could be sitting at home, drinking a beer..."

"... drinking an iced tea," I interrupted.

"Whatever," Harry said. "I don't want to jump out of a plane. Are you kidding me?"

"You bailed on us for the last trip," I reminded him. "You're not getting out of this. We all agreed to do this. Together."

"No, we didn't," Harry argued. "You two bone-heads talked me into joining up, and when I told you I didn't want to risk my life on any unnecessary outings, you said you were okay with that. Both of you."

I looked at Vance and grinned. Neither of us had informed Harry that we wouldn't be jumping. Ordinarily, I wouldn't have let him sweat like this. However, the turkey bailed on us after the rafting trip. He may have avoided bungee jumping, but he wasn't going to get out of this one. "Let's just say we changed our minds."

"I never should have picked up the phone," Harry grumbled to himself. "What was I thinking? Never pick up the phone, especially when you know it's one of these two."

"Is everyone else really undercover cops?" I quietly asked Vance, after Harry had wandered over to the snacks table. "I don't recognize any of them."

Aside from the dozen or so of us Daredevils in the empty airplane hangar, there were also nearly twice that many faces I hadn't seen before, all dressed in matching orange jumpsuits. They were milling about, chatting with each other, with us, and acting like I'd expect a group of young people to act when faced with jumping out of a plane: nervous and excited. As several newcomers wandered close, they smiled at me and then moved off, affording me a look at the logos on their backs. Bend Bravadeers. Cute.

And finally, if I wanted to include all of the people in the hangar, I should mention the staff. Hosting this skydiving event was a company called Pacific NW Jumpers. We were introduced to their staff, who were wearing blue. There were four of them, consisting of three assistants and one pilot. The owner of the company was also there, but then again, he was also our pilot. As I was introduced to each member of the staff, I couldn't help but think that several of them looked familiar, as though I had seen them before. I just couldn't remember where. Whatever. The only thing I cared about was whether Pacific NW Jumpers knew what the hell they were doing.

I nudged Vance and pointed at the orange-suited jumpers.

"Are they all ...?"

"They're on loan from Bend, Medford, and even as far away as Portland," Vance muttered, using a low voice. "Apparently, the Portland cops are still a little sore that this Jerod guy managed to slip away, right from under their noses, too. They were only too happy to extend a helping hand."

Someone I hadn't met before suddenly stepped into the middle of the room and waved an arm, encouraging everyone to gather around him. He was wearing a blue jump suit, which indicated he was one of the staff. Actually, it was the boss.

"Could I have everyone's attention please? Thank you. My name is Art Bullen, and I will be your pilot today. I see that we have a nice, full group, with jumpers hailing from Medford ..."

Every single person wearing an orange jumpsuit whooped loudly while fist-pumping the air.

"... and a last minute addition from Pomme Valley, the Daredevils!"

Vance and I both joined in the chorus of shouts and whistles of all us red-suited Daredevils. Harry, I might add, remained silent. I honestly think, had Vance not been standing between Harry and the door, that our veterinarian friend would make a break for it.

Art nodded. "Right. Okay, with introductions out of the way, let me take a few minutes to point out the refreshment tables behind you. They have an assortment of light snacks, with cups of water available, at no extra charge. I heartily encourage you to have a cup or two. The last thing you want to do is become dehydrated when you're falling through the air at over 120 mph. Take it from someone who has done it before: it's not pleasant. So, please, help yourselves. Fueling is underway and should be done in a minute or two. Thank you."

"He's worried about becoming dehydrated?" I repeated, appalled. "Listen, the only thing I'm worried about is peeing myself on the way down."

Vance chuckled, pulled out his cell phone, and sent off several texts, presumably to Tori and his kids. I decided to take that time to send a few to Jillian. Out of the corner of my eye, I saw Harry edging toward the exit. Vance, without looking up from his phone, took several steps in that direction, which placed him directly in Harry's path once more.

"Come on, man," Harry grumped. "This isn't for me."

"Live a little," Vance said, as he finally looked up. "Look, I'm not going to force you to stay here. I think both Zack and I would like to, but it's beneath us to try. We're here, and we're going through with this. Don't you want to be able to look your family in the eyes and say, hey, I was able to jump out of a perfectly good airplane and not tell them you chickened out?"

Harry's hopeful expression soured. "That was a low blow, man. You both can bite me. Just for that, I'm gonna have an extra cup or two of water. My only request is that you guys follow me on the way down. Hopefully I'll be able to pee on you."

"He's a bright ray of sunshine, isn't he?" Vance snickered. "You gonna get something to drink?"

I shook my head. "I'm good, so I'll pass. That's the last thing I want to worry about on the way down."

"Zack, you do know no one will be jumping, right?" Vance asked, as he lowered his voice down so low I could barely hear him.

"I know. But, for all intents and purposes, we are, so I need to act like I remember that, right?"

Vance shrugged and followed me over to the snacks table. While not interested in the food, I had caught sight of someone I wanted to say hello to. I nudged a young guy on the shoulder and waited for him to turn around. Once he did, Vance's eyes practically bulged out of his head.

It was Ash. Not only had he shaved his beard off, he had his hair styled in such a way that it reminded me of those frosted-tip hairdos found on most boy-band members. I had to hand it to the marshal. Here was someone who was able to commit to a disguise! Pretending we had never met, I held out a hand.

"Hey there. You're one of the Bravadeers? I'm Zack Anderson, and this is Vance Samuelson. We're Daredevils, from Pomme Valley."

"I know who you two are," Ash quietly complained. He was holding one of the cups of water and looked pissed.

"What's the matter?" I quietly asked. "You're not having second thoughts, are you?"

"This isn't going to work," the marshal complained.

Vance gave the people milling about a quick look, as though he was curious to see who else would be jumping with him.

"You must have heard something. Don't keep anything from us, pal."

Ash furtively scratched the side of his face.

"I haven't shaved my beard off in years. Years! I look like I'm twelve years old."

"Your hair style isn't helping," I pointed out.

"I told the stylist I needed something completely different," Ash explained. He scratched the top of his head, felt the gel-hardened clumps his hair had become, and sighed. "I needed to step out of my comfort zone."

"Mission accomplished," Vance chuckled. "Look, there's Thor. I think we're about to get underway."

"Are your people ready for this?" Ash quietly asked. "And I think you two need to call me by something other than my real name."

"How about Justin?" I innocently asked, as I eyed the marshal's hair once more.

"Kiss my patootie," Ash growled. "Detective, you're up. That's the signal."

I glanced back at Thor, and saw he was rubbing his hands together, as though he was cold. Ash was right. It was the agreed upon signal for Vance to make his announcement about having a strong, viable suspect for the two Daredevil deaths.

Vance then whipped out his cell, as though he had received a call. He pretended to talk on it as he paced up and down the length of the snack table. After several minutes had passed, Vance hurried over to the leader of the Daredevils, tapped his shoulder, and whispered something in his ear. Thor looked back at Vance, nodded, and put two fingers in his mouth. A split second later, an ear-splitting whistle ripped through the air.

"Daredevils! Have I got some news for you!

Clouseau here ..."

I chuckled softly as I watched Vance roll his eyes at hearing his 'Devils name.

"... has just informed me he'd like to make an announcement. If you'd all give him your attention, then I'm sure you'll be thanking him afterward."

"Ladies and gentlemen," Vance formally began. "As you may or may not know, I am, in fact, a detective with the Pomme Valley Police Department. I've just been given some news that I think the lot of you deserve to hear: we're closing in on the person responsible for Hades' and Jitters' deaths."

"It wasn't an accident?" Dagger slowly repeated. The young, dark-skinned woman threw her empty cup in the trash and looked up at Thor. "You said it was just an accident. Is there something you're not telling us?"

"There's a better than average chance that someone was responsible for sabotaging Hades' chute," Thor slowly began. "As for Jitters, well ..."

"What about Jitters?" Yeti interrupted. "The raft tipped over. You're telling us that wasn't an accident, either?"

"Oh, the raft tipping over was an accident," Thor confirmed, "only ..."

"Only what?" another voice demanded. I had to lean around Harry to see who had spoken. It was the pale woman who looked, dressed, sounded, and was named after a member of the Addams family: Wednesday.

Thor looked at Vance. "Clouseau? Would you care to field this one?"

Vance solemnly nodded. "While the official cause of Jitters' death was drowning, the medical examiner has confirmed the existence of contusions on her shoulders and chest."

"Contusions?" TooTall repeated, confused. "What is that, an open wound?"

"Bruising," Yeti translated. "Wait. Are you saying someone pushed Jitters into the water after the raft tipped over?"

Vance shook his head. "You're close, I'm sorry to say. The contusions are more in line with a size 10½ boot."

"Someone stepped on her to hold her underwater?" Dagger exclaimed, outraged. "Who? Tell me you've got a suspect in mind. Tell me you can give me a name. Let's see how this sumbitch can handle a woman who can take care of herself. Give me a name, Clouseau."

There was a chorus of angry shouts. The Daredevils smelled blood, and it had driven them into a frenzy.

I noticed Patch, who had been sitting with his head in his hands, suddenly looked up, and then rose to his feet. The people around him automatically fell silent. Patch walked the dozen or so feet over to Vance and gave him an inscrutable look.

"The person who did this to Jitters? Are you saying they were in the same raft as she was?"

Vance nodded. "I am."

"I was on that raft. Am I a suspect?"

Vance shook his head. "As a matter of fact, no. We already have a suspect and are closing the net on him as we speak."

Hippie and Wednesday joined Patch in glaring at Vance. A few moments later, Yeti appeared by Hippie's left side. Together, they stared at Vance —in silence—until my detective friend was fidgeting and shifting his weight from leg to leg. After a few moments, Vance cleared his throat.

"Look, I realize this is unsettling news, but rest assured, we know where the culprit is. We'll have him in custody in no time."

Dagger stormed over to Hippie and started dangerously eyeing him, Yeti, and any other male within range.

"A man. I should've known it'd be a man. Wednesday? I'm sorry."

"For what?" Wednesday quietly asked.

"For even thinking it could be you."

"I didn't do it!" Patch protested. "You don't think it was me, do you?"

Vance held up both hands in the universally recognized gesture of surrender. He started patting the air.

"People, look. It's an ongoing investigation. I won't jeopardize the case until it has been closed. That's what I'm trying to tell you. We are extremely close to picking up our man. Once we do, you'll be the first to hear about it. Now, who wants to go skydiving?"

There was a chorus of enthusiastic shouts. I noticed the pilot, Art, slip out the side door. A few moments later, the twin turbines of the CASA C-212 roared to life. As we filed out of the hangar and stepped outside, we were handed helmets and had our harnesses checked by one of the suited professionals. Only when it passed whatever safety check they were looking for, were we allowed to walk up the large exit ramp located on the rear of the plane. Instead of finding rows of seats like you would in a commercial airliner, the seats on this plane lined the wall on either side of the plane. Completing the picture were five-point harnesses for each seat. I'm also ashamed to say I needed Vance to show me how to hook everything where it needed to go.

I followed Harry, who grudgingly followed Vance, up into the belly of the plane. We took our seats, strapped ourselves in (with Vance's help), and waited for the rest of the jumpers to join us. Since the Daredevils were outfitted in red jumpsuits, and the Bravadeers were in orange, we made quite a colorful contrast to the dull green interior of the plane.

The lead instructor appeared on the ramp, followed by one of his assistants. They buckled themselves in and then each of them gave a thumbs-up. After a few moments, there was a loud grating noise and the exit ramp slowly lifted until it closed with a loud bang. I looked over at Harry and grinned at him.

"Doesn't this remind you of high school?"

"We never were stupid enough to try something like this in high school," Harry reminded me. His eyes were screwed shut and his face had beads of sweat trickling down his forehead.

"I'm talking about going out, after dark, and pulling crazy pranks."

"None were this crazy," Harry argued.

"What about the time when you wanted to be the next MTV star and you *borrowed*," I said, adding air quotes around the word, "the school's VHS camcorder? Do you remember what happened?"

Harry grinned. "Uh, yeah. I kinda got the cops called on me."

Vance perked up. "What? Why? What did you do?"

"He thought it'd be a good idea to film a music video with his BB gun," I explained. "He thought he could be a bad-ass rapper. What was the result? The police were called because they were getting complaints of a kid holding a gun, breakdancing in the street. Ring any bells?"

Vance looked at Harry and shook his head. "You didn't."

"Guilty, man," Harry admitted.

"Breakdancing?" Vance snorted, between chuckles. "That's priceless."

"And what about the time you stole your mom's Honda and drove to the school to sneak into the snack bar?"

Harry looked thoughtful for a moment. "Umm, which time, bro?"

"The time you stole the snacks and drinks, tried to make it back over the fence, but the bag was too heavy? You dropped it on the school-side of the fence and still got caught."

"You mean you went to all that trouble and still didn't get your snacks?" Vance dryly asked.

Harry shrugged. "Should've left the sodas behind."

"Tell him what happened next," I chuckled.

"What happened next?" Vance wanted to know.

"What are you talking about?" Harry asked.

"Where did the police end up going?" I pressed.

Harry grinned. "Oh. That. Well, we had just moved, and unfortunately, the police thought we still lived at the old address. They woke up those neighbors, who were like, 'Oh, they live around the corner now.' It was funny."

"Remind me what your dad did to you?" I teased.

"He might've grounded me for a month," Harry admitted.

"And then?" I innocently asked.

"Took away my car keys."

"And then?"

"Made me apologize to the principal."

"What then ...?"

"Made me work in the cafeteria's lunch line for an entire semester."

"Harsh," Vance decided, but at least he was smiling.

"At least he was able to graduate," I said.

Harry shrugged again, leaned back, and closed his eyes.

As the plane ascended higher and higher into the sky, I entertained myself by watching the passing clouds through the window. Light, wispy clouds coated the windows with tiny droplets of water, which were then whisked away by the passing wind, leaving tiny trails. I looked back at the rest of the people in the plane. Some appeared to be getting some rest. Others were quietly talking among themselves. I looked over at Vance, but he was checking something on his phone.

Right about then, I heard it. Snoring, and it was coming from my left. Curious, I looked over at Harry. Sure enough, his head was tilted back, his mouth was open, and a line of drool was coating the corner of his beard. I tapped Vance's knee and, once he was looking at me, nodded my head toward Harry. Vance studied our friend's still form for a few moments before Harry softly snorted and resumed snoring. Vance chuckled and went back to his phone.

Curious to see what the marshal was doing, I glanced to my right. His head was leaning forward, and I swear, if it wasn't for the complex harness holding him in place, he would have toppled forward. Talk about your heavy sleeper.

As I scanned the faces of my fellow jumpers, I

couldn't help but think that maybe we had this wrong. I didn't see anyone doing anything suspicious. I didn't see anyone nervously glancing about. I mean, I'm not sure what I thought I'd see, but I did at least think I'd see something worth reporting. Instead, all I got was a few thumbs-up from several nearby jumpers.

The plane must have hit a rough patch of turbulence just then, because it suddenly felt like I was being tightly gripped by a giant, who then proceeded to shake me, as though I was a bottle of soda pop. The shaking might have only lasted for a few seconds, but wow, was I gonna be feeling that tomorrow.

I heard another series of snores. Surprised, I glanced back at Harry. The poor guy was still out. I then looked over at Ash and was equally surprised to see that he, too, was fast asleep. I was reminded of one of my favorite movies, Aliens, and the character of Hicks, who during the descent to LV-426, had promptly fallen asleep. Michael Biehn's character had to be woken up by his commanding officer prior to their arrival. This, strangely enough, reminded me of that.

"I'm surprised anyone could sleep through that," I heard Vance say.

I glanced over and saw him looking at Harry.

"I've been told I can sleep anywhere, but had I felt something like that, I'd be looking for a new pair of underwear."

Vance laughed, and started to pull his phone

back out when he paused. He slowly scanned the nearby jumpers and, with a surprised look on his face, turned back to me.

"What is it?" I wanted to know.

Vance pointed at the nearby jumpers. "Zack, they're asleep, too."

"So? Some people can sleep on planes."

"After that turbulence? There's no way. Look at them, pal. They're all asleep."

An eerie feeling washed over me as I pivoted (as much as I could in the harness) to study the other occupants of the plane. Vance was right. They were all asleep. I looked at the bobbing heads, the limp, lifeless arms, and the swaying legs (for those not tall enough to reach the floor) and looked back at my friend.

"Dude, what the hell is going on? Am I the only one who's creeped out by this?"

"Something's wrong," Vance decided. "We need to alert the pilot. Is ... is Justin awake?"

I looked over at the marshal and had to shake my head. Ash was just as out of it as the rest of the jumpers.

"Justin?" a new voice sneered. "How cute. Let Marshal Binson sleep, would you? What I have to say is not for his ears."

Surprised, both Vance and I slowly turned to look for the speaker. One other Daredevil was awake, and was standing before us, holding a gun. He was wearing a victorious look on his face as he stood over us, brandishing his weapon.

"Expecting someone else?" Jafo sneered.

TEN

There's no way it could be you," Vance protested. "You're too tall! We were told you were only five-six. There's no way the marshal would've been off by half a foot."

Jafo, otherwise known as Jerod Jones, looked over at the sleeping form of Ash Binson, and gave him a piteous shake of the head. "Our friend, the marshal, is not the most observant of people. Did you know that, if you hunch your back, bend your knees, and slouch, you can shave inches off your height? It's the easiest thing in the world to do, yet Marshal Binson never once caught on." Jerod leveled the gun at us and frowned. "I overheard him once tell an associate that he thought I had MS. Idiot. Now, tell me how you two knew not to drink the water."

"Wasn't thirsty," Vance replied, keeping his voice calm and neutral.

"Neither was I," I admitted.

Jerod shook his head. "I don't buy it. Look around. Everyone else drank the water. Why wouldn't you? You clearly knew something was wrong with it. So, how did you know it had been spiked?"

"How did you spike it?" I asked, confused. "You were sitting out in the open the entire time we were in that hangar. You didn't have time to spike each and every cup. You had to have done it earlier."

Jerod grinned nastily at us, but refused to answer.

Vance grunted, "Good point, Zack. How did he manage it?"

Jerod groaned. "Oh, of course. This is the part where I disclose all my activities, my plans, and secrets as to why I've done what I've done."

"Why did you spike the water?" Vance wanted to know.

"Isn't it obvious?" I asked, as I turned to my friend. "He knows about them."

Vance glared at Jerod, as if daring him to confirm the allegation. To his credit, Jerod didn't say anything. Vance looked at me, sneered once in Jerod's direction, and then nodded his head.

"Told you he didn't know. It was just a fluke coincidence."

"Coincidence?" Jerod angrily repeated. "Look around you, Detective Samuelson. Do you see any of your backup here? Awake, that is?"

"Told you he knows," I moaned. "Although, how you figured that out is a mystery to me."

"Oh, please," Jerod scoffed. "I knew about your scheme to ... how did you put it, detective? Flush me out? I learned about this plan of yours yester-day."

"Yesterday?" Vance slowly repeated? "That's when the plan was formulated. How could you possibly know we were planning on outing you?"

Jerod looked over at Ash's prone form and sighed. "You people must really think I'm an im-becile. I recognized Marshal Binson the moment he arrived in town. I knew immediately what he was there to do. It wasn't hard to learn his move-ments and what he knew. Hell, he told me himself that he was there to apprehend a missing fugi-tive."

I looked over at Ash and groaned. "You're kid-ding."

"What'd he tell you?" Jerod wanted to know. "That he was in town, looking to find out where I was hiding?"

"He said he didn't know what disguise you'd be hiding under," I sullenly confirmed.

"Disguise?" Jerod chortled, with glee. "What disguise?"

"He said you were good with disguises," I re-called. "He said you could be anyone."

"Do you think the absence of a disguise could be considered a disguise?" Jerod thoughtfully asked. Then he grinned like a bully who knows he has the upper hand. "I knew he was dumb, but this takes the cake. How he became a marshal is simply beyond me."

"What do you mean?" I asked, not certain if I

wanted to know the answer.

"He's seen my face!" Jerod explained, as he tapped the side of his head. "I was his prisoner, up in Portland. Does he not trust his own two eyes?"

"You did disappear right under his nose," I pointed out.

"Is that what he told you?" Jerod exclaimed, as he rocked back and forth with delight. "I had no idea I made such an impression on him."

"You're not fooling anyone with this song and dance," Vance matter-of-factly said. "We know you're a quick-change artist. I'll bet you can't pull a fast one on me."

"I already have," Jerod cried, as tears of laughter rolled down his face. "Haven't you figured it out yet? How else could I have known so much about your precious plan? How could I have possibly known you were working my case with Marshal Dumbass here?"

"I know you're not a cop," Vance argued. "I can only assume that someone privy to the plan announced it over the radio, and you heard it on a police scanner."

"Wrong again," Jerod cheerfully gloated.

"The only way you could have known," I began, as the pieces to this complex puzzle started falling into place, "would be if you were physically present when we were going over the details. I can't speak for Vance, but I sure as hell didn't see you anywhere. We were at the hospital when we were talking with Ash about the case."

"Outside," Vance clarified. "We were talking with him outside."

I nodded. "That's right. There was no one else there. No one else but ... holy cow. You were there, weren't you?"

Jerod bowed once to me and started clapping.

"Bravo. At least one of you isn't an idiot."

"You're suggesting you were at the hospital and overheard us talking?" Vance shook his head. "I'm not buying it."

"Whether or not you *buy* anything isn't my concern," Jerod coldly stated. Gone was the smug visage he had adopted from the moment he revealed himself. Gone were the condescending looks and eye rolls. "You people are all pathetic. I walked right by the four of you. You had asked our friend, the marshal, whether or not he had an angle he was working for the case. As it turns out, he didn't."

"Impossible," Vance breathed. "If what you say is true, then I must be as blind as a bat. I didn't see anyone else."

"Yet, clearly, I was there" Jerod sneered.

"There's no way," Vance whispered.

"How'd you do it?" I curiously asked. "You must have found a way to move around undetected, only I have no idea what that could be."

"Think harder, Bacchus," Jerod challenged. "You're the writer, so figure it out."

"You know I'm a writer?" I echoed, amazed.

"Because you told me you were. Good God,

man. We were in the Daredevils together. You stood up and announced what you did to the entire group. Is your short-term memory really that bad?"

"Bite me," I scowled. "Wait. You say you were at the hospital?"

Jerod grinned. "Obviously."

"If I'm right about this, then you've also been to the police station, too," I guessed.

Jerod beamed a smile and bowed. "But of course."

A notion dawned.

"Who has the ability to move from place to place, and pretty much become invisible to everyone present?" I asked Vance.

"Don't you start, too," Vance groaned. "No more riddles. If I knew, then I'd … the janitor! You were posing as the damn janitor. You're the one who emptied the mop bucket in the parking lot the day we were there for C2, weren't you?"

"With pride. People say the damnedest things when they think there's no one listening. You may as well be invisible if you're pushing a mop bucket. As for you and your investigation, well, after I heard you go over your plan at the police station, I knew what had to be done. On top of that, Marshal Dumbass himself shows up, along with Tweedle-Dee and Tweedle-Dum? You don't have to be a rocket scientist to figure out what's going on."

"If you knew all these extra cops were going to

be here," I hesitantly began, "and this was nothing but a trap, then why bother showing up? Why not simply disappear, like you've done before?"

Jerod idly scratched his chin. "Well, you guys put so much thought and effort into this endeavor that it would be a shame to let it go to waste. Why mess up all of your hard work?"

"Arrogant little putz," I heard Vance growl.

A thought occurred, and as long as Jerod was being so talkative, perhaps he'd shed some light on the matter.

"Look, Jerod, would you answer a couple of questions for me?"

"If I feel like it," Jerod smirked. His gun was still pointed at Vance, although it wasn't aimed at his chest anymore.

"How did you pull off Jitters' death? I mean, you weren't even in the same raft. I saw you. You were sitting up front, in the first one. You guys didn't go over that Class IV."

Jerod waved the gun, as if to encourage me to rapidly come to the point.

"That would mean you'd have to be in the water in order to hold Jitters down, beneath the water," I continued.

"Using your boot," Vance added.

"I'll bet you'd like for me to comment on that one," Jerod teased, glancing over at the detective.

"What harm could it do to tell us?" I innocently asked. "You're gonna be jumping off this plane shortly, aren't you? You're going to make a successful escape. Surely, there's no harm in telling."

"He's not responsible," Vance decided. "He just couldn't be."

"Says who?" Jerod laughed. "I must admit, this is highly entertaining. I'm having the time of my life with you two. Thank you for that."

"You think you've outsmarted us," I began, "so …"

"I have outsmarted you," Jerod proudly stated. "I've outsmarted everyone."

"Then prove it," I countered. "You're clearly responsible for Jitters' death. How'd you pull it off?"

"How do you think I pulled it off?" Jerod politely asked.

"You were on the first raft," I recalled. "Assuming you got off the raft and watched the proceedings with everyone else, then there's no way you could have snuck away. Hell, Vance and I were there. So … that means you couldn't have been the person who held Jitters underwater."

Jerod cocked his head and smiled, but refrained from saying anything.

"You have an accomplice," Vance groaned. "Son of a bitch. I should have picked up on that."

"Yes, you should have," Jerod gloated.

"Marshal Binson said there were no known associates," I reminded Vance. I looked back at Jerod. "Who is it? We know it wasn't your former roommate. You killed him several months ago."

"Then, who could it be?" Jerod innocently asked. "What's your guess?"

I looked at Vance, who shrugged. I think my detective friend was too pissed off to play Jerod's little game. As for me, well, I wanted answers. As long as he was willing to talk, I was willing to play along.

"Let's think about this," I began. "You obviously don't care about your former friend, so why else would you have come here, to Pomme Valley?"

"Why, indeed?" Jerod asked, still grinning that irritating smile of his.

I mentally reviewed the third raft as it dropped over the Class IV rapid when we all went rafting. Of the five Daredevils aboard the raft, four were able to escape, leaving Jitters and … the guide! It had to be the river guide, but why? Why would he be willing to commit murder for the sake of a convicted killer? What hold could Jerod possibly have over him?

Or … could the link between killer and guide be something more? Like, I don't know … maybe a familial connection?

I pulled up what I could remember of the guide's face and compared it to Jerod's. Could the two of them be related? I remember thinking one or more of the staff looked familiar.

Just then, I flashed back to meeting the staff members who were assisting the skydivers for our two groups. I remembered thinking one of them looked familiar. Well, now I know why. I had seen one of the Pacific NW Jumpers before. He had been introduced to us as Robert, only I knew him as Jason, the river rat from the third raft! I pictured Jerod, standing next to Jason, and compared the two. Same height, which I originally disregarded. Same hair color. Same nose. That meant ...

"I can see it in your eyes," Jerod praised. "Good job. You're clearly the brains of this outfit."

"You can see what in his eyes?" Vance curiously asked. My friend turned to me. "What is it? What aren't you sharing?"

"I know why Jerod came to PV," I proudly declared.

Vance was astonished. "You do? How? Why?"

I turned to look at Jerod. "Marshal Binson's information was incomplete. He said there were no known relatives. Well, he's missing one: your father. We know him as Jason, the river rat."

Vance frowned. "The river guide? He's Jerod's father? No, I don't buy it."

I looked at Jerod. "Tell him."

Jerod shrugged. "He's my father."

Vance whistled. "I'll be a monkey's uncle. I wouldn't have called that one. So, are you telling me your father is the one who killed Jitters?"

"When the raft tipped over, yes."

"What kind of a messed-up family did you come from?" I incredulously asked. "Since when would a father willingly kill for his son?"

"What father wouldn't want to keep his son out of jail?" Jerod countered.

I snapped my fingers. "The guy in the camouflage pants! That was your dad, wasn't it?"

Jerod blinked at me, with confusion written all over his face.

"What was that?"

"Your father," I continued. "When he's not in disguise, does he usually wear camouflage pants?"

Jerod shrugged. "At times. Why? How would you know that?"

"I've seen him in PV," I admitted. "And, I'm pretty sure I saw him when we were all bungee jumping."

Jerod hissed with annoyance. "I told him to lay low and remain concealed. There's someone else who doesn't follow directions."

Vance groaned. "Directions? Your father is the person who spiked the water today, isn't he?"

Jerod nodded. "Yep. It was my idea, though. Dad wanted to know how I was planning on escaping. Told him a little GHB goes a long way."

"A little what?" I asked, confused.

"You used liquid ecstasy on them?" Vance demanded. "Just how the hell did you get your hands on that?"

"Wouldn't you like to know," Jerod sneered.

I held my hands in a time-out gesture. "Just what is GHB? Is it as bad as it sounds?"

"GHB is short for gamma-hydroxybutyric acid," Vance reported, as if he was reciting the explanation from a medical encyclopedia. "It's illegal as hell."

"So, sue me," Jerod chuckled. He pointedly

looked at the sleeping people still snoring in their seats. "It worked, didn't it? Dad did a great job."

"What did your father have against Jitters?" I asked, confused. "What sob story could you have possibly cooked up that would have convinced him to do your bidding?"

"Jitters was Jim's girlfriend," Jerod coldly replied. "She had spent time at our apartment, with me and Jim. She was starting to see through my disguise."

Vance's mouth dropped open. "Jitters was Jim's girlfriend. I never caught that."

"Jim?" I repeated, confused.

"The roommate," Vance explained. "James. Hades? Any of this ring a bell?"

I nodded. "*That* James. Okay. What about C2? What'd he do to you? Did he find out who you really are?"

Jerod gave a noncommittal shrug. "I don't really have anything against C2."

"Then, why'd you do it?" Vance asked.

Jerod suddenly grinned. "Honestly? I didn't mean to. It was dark. I grabbed the wrong harness."

"Whose did you want?" Vance asked.

Jerod shrugged. "Either of you two would've made me happy."

As I eyed Vance, to see what his reaction to that would be, Jerod reached into his jacket pocket and pulled something out. I heard the tell-tale crinkle of a plastic wrapper and realized he must have pulled out some type of snack. Once Jerod turned back around, and I saw what was in his hand, I shook my head.

"What?" Jerod demanded.

"Nothing," I decided. "Have you always liked Zingers?"

Jerod looked down at the snack cake with the thick frosting on top and shrugged.

"Call it a weakness. I've always had a thing for these."

"You like the sugar rush," Vance guessed.

Jerod shrugged again, but then frowned when he saw me look conspiratorially at Vance.

"What?" he demanded. The gun swung around until it was pointed at us. Well, me, in particular.

"Nothing," I said. "Seeing you with that Zinger has answered a few questions for me."

"Like?" Jerod challenged.

"Your fascination with convenience stores for one," Vance answered.

"What about them?" Jerod curiously asked.

"You break out of prison, but then promptly hold up a convenience store?" I asked, as I recalled the information Ash had given us when we had first met. "You were going after those sugar bombs, weren't you?"

Jerod grinned, and took a healthy bite of his snack cake. Stuffing the last bit of icing and cake into his mouth, he immediately reached for the second of three cakes in the package.

"The grocery store," I reminded Vance. "What do you want to bet he was trying to draw our attention to the store?"

Vance looked over at me. "Huh?"

"Whenever we were out driving around? And we got a reaction from the dogs whenever we passed the grocery store? They were trying to alert us to these damn mini cakes."

Vance nodded. "I can buy that. Do you think that goes for the gas station, too?"

At this point, we were completely ignoring the convicted mass murderer—holding the gun—and, instead, having a quick, cheerful comparison of notes, like we would if we were talking about our favorite football teams. Understandably, this did not go over well with the aforementioned mass murderer. Jerod strode purposely up to me and thrust the gun in my face.

"Do I look like someone who should be crossed?"

"Oh. Sorry 'bout that. Look, I'm just saying that we were aware of your visits to the grocery store and the gas station. Now we know it's because of those things. Seriously, man, are you sure you want to keep eating those? They are, what, a thousand calories a piece?"

Having finished the second cake in the package, Jerod moved to the third. He slowly crumpled the wrapper up and then tucked it inside Ash's jumpsuit.

"Why do I get the feeling we aren't gonna like what happens when he finishes that last cake?" Vance quietly asked.

Jerod grunted once and held the gun up, like he was making a toast.

"We need to keep him talking," I softly murmured. And, seeing how Jerod didn't appear to like knowing we knew about his habits, inspiration struck. "How long were you at that campsite?"

Jerod paused, with the Zinger only halfway to his mouth.

"What?"

"How long were you at that campsite by the river?" I repeated.

"Wh-what campsite?" Jerod stammered.

Vance and I shared another conspiratorial look. "You know exactly which one I mean. It had the small, built-in barbecue, with the two picnic tables nearby?"

"You're bluffing. Grasping at straws, are you?"

I looked over at Vance. "What was it, maybe half a mile from that Class IV drop?"

"Upriver," Vance confirmed.

"I was there two days ago," Jerod quietly confirmed.

"Researching the river, no doubt," Vance deduced.

"How did you find it?" Jerod asked.

I shrugged. "Does it matter?"

Just like that, I was staring at the business end of Jerod's gun. Again. "How did you find it, writer? I told no one about it."

I became worried that, should I tell Jerod about Sherlock and Watson, that he might seek retaliation against them for being able to figure out what he'd been up to. So, I wasn't about to tell him a damn thing. Vance, noting the look of resolve which had appeared on my face, nodded his agreement. The gun suddenly swung over to Vance.

"One of you, and I don't care who, is going to tell me how you knew about that campsite."

To this day, I still have no idea what came over me there, in the plane. The only thing I remember, at the time, was thinking there was no way Jerod was going to let Vance and me leave with our lives. Why, then, should I tell him a damn thing? The answer was simple: I won't.

"No, I don't think so."

"I'm the one holding the gun here," Jerod reminded me, as he waggled the gun directly in my face. "You'll do as I say or ..."

"Or what?" I wanted to know, as I threw as much of a sneer in my voice as I could. "You'll kill me? Logic suggests you're already planning on doing that. Anyone can see it."

"Well, if you want to live, then you'd better do as you're told," Jerod sputtered, growing angry.

"Nope."

"Nope?" Jerod incredulously repeated. He looked at Vance, as though he couldn't believe someone had the gall to refuse him.

My friend shrugged and ended up nodding. "I'm with him. I don't feel like cooperating, either. If you're going to shoot us, then just do it and get it over with."

Jerod seethed with frustration, and for one horrifying moment, I actually thought he might take Vance up on that very notion. Then, an evil smile appeared on his face, and I knew he had, somehow, found another ace up his sleeve. From the way he was leering at the sleeping passengers, I knew it wasn't gonna be good.

"Don't even think it," I warned him. "There are over two dozen people on this plane."

Jerod fell silent.

"You've won, buddy," Vance added. "You outsmarted everyone. You've got the gun, you've got a parachute, and you have the advantage. Just jump and go, all right?"

"Oh, I will. But, here's the thing. You two will be joining me."

Vance and I both shook our heads no.

"Methinks not, amigo," I contradicted.

"You're not going to jump?" Jerod asked, then frowned. "After all we've been through, you don't want to make that final jump?"

"Absolutely not," I said.

"I'll pass," Vance said, at the same time.

"I think you will," Jerod argued.

"I think you're wrong," Vance argued. "Why the hell would either of us jump now?"

"Oh, you're clearly not intimidated by the notion of death, so this will be a piece of cake. Besides, you two are inexperienced. This will be fun as hell to watch."

"You can get your kicks elsewhere," I staunchly

declared.

My heart sank as Jerod's gun, which had been pointed at Vance, suddenly swung around and stopped. At the cockpit.

"You will jump, or I'll shoot the pilot."

"You can't do that!" Vance cried. "Think of the people here. They'd all die!"

"Then prepare yourself, Clouseau," Jerod snapped. He pulled back his left sleeve to study his watch. "I'd hurry if I were you. You have less than two minutes until we're jumping."

"Jumping out of this plane was never part of the plan," I argued.

Jerod eyed the parachutes Vance and I were wearing and whistled. "You already have the chutes. Seems to me it'd be a shame if we didn't use them."

"And even if I was willing," I continued to argue (I really don't know why I continued to protest), "which I'm not, there's no one to do a tandem jump with me."

Jerod leered at me. "Nice try. You're too big for a tandem jump. Besides, if you were really planning on a tandem jump, then you wouldn't be wearing a parachute, would you? Your instructor would. You were going to use a static line, and you know it."

Well, it was worth a try.

"Fine. I'll use the static line."

"Not this time, Bacchus. You'll jump when I say to jump, otherwise this plane will be in for a very rough landing."

I looked back at the unconscious form of Harry, then Ash, and all the members of the Daredevils and the police officers who had volunteered for this mission. I couldn't let them come to any harm. Whether I liked it or not, I was gonna have to do this.

"If we do this," I nervously began, as I began tugging on my parachute's shoulder straps, to tighten them as much as I could, "how do we know you'll allow these people to safely land?"

Jerod returned to his seat to pull out the helmet stored in a bag, comprised of netting, underneath. He strapped it to his head and pulled the goggles down over his eyes.

"You don't. But, don't worry. We're all going to jump together."

"No, we're not," a new voice suddenly announced.

I turned to see who had spoken and almost danced with joy. It was Marshal Binson, and he was holding a gun! I had to stop myself from fist-pumping the air. Much to my dismay, however, Jerod didn't seem too surprised.

"Well, well, Sleeping Beauty has finally awoken."

"I was never asleep," Ash pointed out. "I had to wait for you to identify yourself. I must admit, you don't look like you usually do."

Jerod opened his arms wide, "This is me, all right, in the flesh. I must admit, I didn't think you'd wake back up."

"I told you," Ash all but growled, "I wasn't asleep."

"Your body language says otherwise," Jerod replied.

It was at this time that I noticed Ash's gun was not pointed at Ash, but at a point somewhere to the left of where Jerod was standing. Wasn't he worried that he'd punch a hole through the aircraft? And clearly Jerod was unconcerned. Did he know something we didn't?

"Your face has sleep lines, your hair is tousled, and your eyes are dilated. No, Marshal Dumbass, you were asleep. That tells me you're still drugged."

"Am not," Ash insisted.

And … it was at this time that Ash's gun wavered and moved a little to the right, as though the marshal had noticed his aim was off. However, he was now too far to the right. Of all the infernal luck. Jerod was right. Ash had somehow regained consciousness, but that didn't mean he was in full control of his faculties. Add a firearm to the mix, and you have a recipe for disaster.

"You see it, don't you?" Jerod said, directed to me. "And you? Clouseau? Love the name, by the way. What's your professional take on Marshal Dumbass here?"

I could see that it didn't take long for Vance to determine Ash had no business standing in a shaking plane, such as this. In fact, the turbulence was starting to get worse, which prompted Vance to release himself from his seat belt and head toward the marshal. Vance sighed heavily and then pointed at the closest seat.

"You'd better have a seat, pal. You're in no condition to ..."

"Don't presume to tell me what to do," Ash snapped. His gaze was unfocused, and the gun had started to shake. "I'm taking this scumbag in, and that's final."

We must have hit a rough patch of air, because all of a sudden, the plane was shaking so bad that all of us were thrown off balance. Well, Vance, Ash, and Jerod were. They were all thrown together and went down in a tumble of arms and legs. As for me? Well, I was still strapped in to my seat. Grumbles and curses were tossed about as Jerod hastily extricated himself from underneath Vance and Ash. His gun was immediately pointed at the cockpit.

"Both of you, on your feet," Jerod growled, as he stepped to his right so he'd be in line with the cockpit. "If either of you so much as twitch, then I'm going to send a bullet straight through our pilot's brain pan. Care to guess what'll happen to everyone here?"

Ash blinked a few times as his befuddled brain tried to process Jerod's threat.

"We don't want that to happen," I said, stepping in. The turbulence had died down, so I finally released myself from my seat. "Listen, pal, this is gonna have to be the one who got away. There's too much at stake here."

"I cannot let him go," Ash vehemently declared. "If he takes out the pilot, I can guarantee you he'll be dead before he can take another shot."

"You're talking about the pilot," Vance tried to point out. "Unless you can fly this bird and, I'm guessing by your condition, you can't, you have to let him go."

"And we're supposed to take your word that you'll leave these people alone?" Ash argued. "What about your father? Where's he been hiding? How do I know he won't be waiting for them back at the hangar?"

Jerod checked his watch again and stepped over to a small, square panel. It contained two buttons: green and red. He stabbed his finger down on the green button. Even though it was unbelievably loud inside the plane, we could still hear the groaning metal as the plane's exit ramp began to lower.

"You won't. I could tell you my father will be waiting for me on the ground, and you might believe me. Or you might not. Either way, I don't care. Now, Clouseau? Bacchus? Get ready."

Confused, Ash looked at me and Vance and cocked his head. "Where are you guys going?"

"We're apparently going skydiving," Vance groaned.

I held up my hands in another time out. "Wait a damn minute! How am I supposed to know when to pull the handle? How am I supposed to steer this thing? I don't know how to do any of that!"

Jerod was shaking his head. He pointed the gun back at the two of us and nodded toward the ramp. Out of the corner of my eye, I could see Ash's face redden with anger. Jerod was completely ignoring him, as though he were no more dangerous than a guinea pig.

"They're not going anywhere," Ash insisted. He aimed his gun. "Neither are you, Jerod Jones."

"At least point the gun at me, and not at one of your undercover officers," Jerod complained, as he turned his back on the marshal and adjusted the parachute straps around his legs.

Surprised, Ash looked down at his gun, then in Jerod's direction. "I *am* pointing it at you."

"Actually, you're not," I quietly told the marshal. "Trust me, I'm impressed as hell you managed to wake up, but you clearly are not fully awake. Put the gun down before you hurt someone besides Jerod."

Ash turned to Vance. "Is he serious?"

"He is. There's no shame in sitting this one out, Marshal."

Marshal Binson's gun lowered, until it was pointing down.

"Good boy," Jerod said, as though he was praising a five-year-old. "Now, are the senior citizens ready?"

I looked over at Vance, back at the exit ramp, and then down at the teeny tiny checkerboard the ground had become, thousands of feet below.

"I'm really wishing I had gone to the bathroom right about now," I groaned.

Just before the three of us could step off the exit ramp and out into nothing but air, Jerod turned, tossed the gun to Ash, and waved.

"See ya on the other side, Marshal!"

With that, Jerod pushed the two of us out of the plane and then followed us out.

ELEVEN

The movies had it all wrong. How many times have you watched someone jump out of a plane and then have a friendly conversation with the person next to them as they tumbled—end over end—through the air? Well, take it from me. It doesn't work that way, not in the real world. The wind was rushing by me so damn fast that I didn't have a snowball's chance in hell of hearing anything, let alone hear my own screaming, which I'm sure I was doing.

I looked at my flailing arms and legs and realized that freaking out and panicking—in mid-air—was completely pointless. After all, I did have a parachute on. All I had to do was pull the cord and then pray I didn't drift into some power lines on the way down.

Yes, that's a morbid thought to have, but then again, I was just forced out of a plane at gun point. A little bit of rational reasoning was much better than losing my cool, which based on Vance's frantic arm movements, was exactly what he was doing. A split second later, his parachute opened, and he was violently yanked skyward.

Remembering we had a third member of our party, I quickly scanned the skies for Jerod, but I couldn't see him anywhere. True to his word, the worst mass murderer to ever grace Pomme Valley with his presence had made good on his escape.

Whatever. Right now, I had more pressing problems to deal with. Vance had the right idea. It was time to bring this nightmarish freefall to an abrupt end.

My fingers had just located the handle and had closed around it, and I was ready to pull, when I caught sight of a distant form, tumbling end over end as if he was an out-of-control airplane caught in a spin. What had happened to Jerod? Had he somehow knocked himself out when he jumped out of the plane?

The mists cleared, and the cloud I had been falling through finally dissipated. That was when I caught sight of a second distant object. This figure had his arms and legs tucked tightly to his sides, and he was angled away from us, which explained why the distance between us had been steadily increasing. Who, then, was this fourth person?

My hand refused to pull the handle. I don't know why. I sure as hell gave it the order, since falling like this was—in my opinion—anything but fun. But, something was nagging me. Something felt … off. Whoever that person was, it was clear they were in trouble.

Then it hit me. Son of a bitch. Only one person

was stupid enough to follow us out of that plane, especially drugged. It was Ash--it had to be. However, it looked like the sensation of falling had caused the marshal to pass out. If he wasn't awake to pull the cord on his parachute, then how the hell was he expected to walk away from this experience?

Jerod was gone. Vance had deployed his parachute. Ash was unconscious. That left only one person: Yours Truly.

"You've got to be kidding me," I shouted, at the top of my lungs.

It didn't do any good. The winds whipped the words out of my mouth the second they were spoken. No wonder we were told to keep ourselves hydrated. The simple act of speaking resulted in a bone-dry mouth in less than two seconds.

A quick glance at the ground confirmed I had about five minutes before I would become a human hamburger patty, so if I was really going to do something, then it had to be now. The problem was, how do I get over to him? Ash had to be several hundred feet away, and at least a couple hundred feet higher than me.

This is where my love of movies comes in. Now this? This part I've seen, numerous times, and the physics do hold up. Spreading your arms and legs, like Da Vinci's Vitruvian Man, would create more drag, and therefore, partially slow your descent.

Yes! It was working! Ash's spinning form was

getting closer. By twisting this way and that, and then mimicking the straight-as-an-arrow form I had seen Jerod use, I was able to get close enough to Ash where I could reach out and snag a leg. Once I had the marshal falling normally, and had stopped the spinning, I ran my hands down his sides, looking for the pull-cord.

Talk about inappropriate as hell. One guy feeling another guy up? *Blech.* But, these were extenuating circumstances.

There! I found the handle, and based on how quickly the ground was approaching, I had less than two minutes before impact. About ready to give the cord a mighty yank, I caught sight of Rascal River, snaking this way and that. Unfortunately, it looked as though we were angling straight for it. And, complicating the matter, trees could be seen lining the river for miles in either direction. This definitely wasn't the time to be landing in the middle of a forest. What was going to happen when we landed? What would happen if Ash landed in the water? He'd drown! Then again, I couldn't imagine hitting the trees would be that much safer.

Steeling myself, I yanked hard on the cord, and was rewarded with seeing Ash's small auxiliary parachute deploy, which snapped open and deployed the main chute. The marshal was yanked out of my grip as his momentum slowed drastically, as it was supposed to do. Eyeing the river below me, I yanked my own cord and waited for my own chute to open. All in all, it only took about three seconds to completely open and yank my sorry butt to what felt like a standstill.

Now I know why the instructors were so keen on making sure the straps and fasteners on our chutes were as tight as possible. The rapid deceleration had to be the most unpleasant experience of the entire excursion (not counting having a gun thrust in my face). And, since the parachute has straps that circle around my thighs, and are all hooked together, I can't even imagine what it'd be like if your freefall was jerked to a stop, and those straps rode up.

Ah! This was more like it! The wind was no longer howling at my face. I could hear birds chirping and leaves rustling as I neared the ground. Unfortunately, I also heard rushing water. A quick check below me confirmed I was headed straight for the river.

"Oh, sure. Why the hell not?"

Thankful to the instructors for pointing out the quick release fastener, so the parachutist wouldn't be dragged along the ground after landing, I released the chute nearly a dozen feet above the river, and just like that, I was back in the Rascal. And it was just as cold as I remembered. Only, this time, there was no raft waiting for me.

The section of river I had been dropped in was blissfully calm, only it didn't stay that way. In fact, I did remember this part of the river from when we rafted it earlier. If memory served, a lateral, or narrowing of the river, was just past those trees, which meant things were about to get a whole lot trickier. It was time to get my fat butt moving!

One thing I didn't count on was how tired I had become. I must have flailed more than I realized, 'cause it felt like I had just spent forty-five minutes on my tread-climber exercise machine. Swimming became a chore, and much to my horror, I realized I wasn't going to make it to shore before the river narrowed.

Less than ten seconds later, I was jetting along in the river, bouncing painfully off of submerged rocks, protruding branches, and any number of other things in the river. My parachute, which had been jettisoned over the water, rushed by me. I don't know why I did it, but I reached out to grab several of the trailing strings and lines.

Thanks to the cold temperature of the water, I felt my body going numb. If I had any hope of rescue, then it was going to fall on my ability to hold on to something in order to be dragged out of the water. Right now, my best bet was my parachute. So, before I lost all feeling in my fingers and hands, I tied the cords around my right hand and prayed it would hold.

A wave of cold water splashed in my face as it suddenly felt like my parachute had become entangled with the propeller of a boat, and I was being pulled through the water. My teeth started chattering, my hands were numb, and the only thing I could think about was the location of that damn Class IV drop-off. Was I close?

"Zack! Jesus! Hold on, buddy!"

I turned to the voice. It was Vance! How had he managed to get on the ground so quickly?

"Grab hold!"

My eyes wouldn't focus, no matter how many times I blinked. Thankfully, my ears still worked, and they told me Vance was scrambling along the riverbank, trying to get ahead of me.

"He's got hold of the chute!" I heard someone else shout. "See that? He's wrapped it around his hand. Someone snag that chute!"

I don't know the exact specifics of what happened next. Vance told me later that night that he and a family of campers he had stumbled across formed a human chain and stretched out far enough to grab the parachute. Since I had tied myself to it, it was just a matter of reeling me in.

"Get him next to the fire," a female voice said.

"I'm o-okay," I managed to get out. Finally free of the water, my eyes cleared. There was a sea of faces—mostly unknowns—staring down at me. A blanket was produced, which Vance flung over my shoulders. "H-how did you g-get down so f-fast?"

"How'd I get down so fast?" Vance repeated, confused. "It took forever to reach the land. I opened my chute too damn early. What happened? Did you see where Jerod went?"

"N-no." Damn chills. My teeth were chattering, and I know I was sounding just like Woody Woodpecker.

"What happened?" Vance wanted to know. "Why'd it take you so damn long to deploy your chute? Jesus, Zack. I thought I had lost you. I never want to feel like that again."

"Where's Ash?" I carefully asked, determined not to stammer.

Vance blinked and stared at me. "Did you just ask me where your ass is? Seriously?"

As serious as the situation was, this drew a laugh not only from me, but from the nearby campers, too.

"N-no. Doofus. Ash. Where's Ash?"

"Probably still in the plane, why?"

"No. He followed us." I took a deep breath and tried to calm my nerves. "The jump knocked him out. I had to pull his cord for him."

Vance's eyes bugged out as he stared at me. The campers, overhearing what I had to do, gasped with alarm. "He's okay. At least, I think he's okay. I'm pretty sure he's up a tree somewhere."

Vance hastily unzipped his red jumpsuit and fumbled about inside, but his hand came back empty.

"Where's your phone?" I asked, concerned. "You didn't drop it, did you?"

Vance looked at the campers. "Does someone have a cell phone I could borrow? It's a police emergency."

I was about ready to volunteer mine when I felt my pockets through the jumpsuit I was wearing. I couldn't feel it anywhere. Had I lost mine, too?

"This is a technology-free trip for us," an older male proudly announced. "It's a way of reconnecting, as a family."

Vance scoffed and looked at the extended family of four adults and five kids. Two of the kids looked as though they were in high school. Vance zeroed in on the girl, a short blonde with an unhappy expression on her face and waggled a finger at her.

"I need to borrow your phone."

"You heard my grandfather," the girl said, as she shook her head. "There are no cell phones allowed on this trip."

"I don't have time to argue this," Vance snapped. "We're after a killer, and he's gonna get away if you don't loan me your phone. Now, please, hand it over."

"But ..." the girl protested.

"There's no way you would have left your phone behind," I added, coming to Vance's aid. I then met the disapproving stares coming from the girl's parents and grandparents. "She's not going to be in trouble, is that understood?"

The girl reluctantly slid a purple, blinged-out cell phone case out of her back pocket and handed it to Vance. Right about then, I remembered I had slid my phone into my jacket's inside pocket. My hands were still too cold to be able to work my jumpsuit's zipper, so I immediately tucked them under my arms. Something was telling me that I was going to need my phone shortly.

"Teresa!" the older man scowled. "You said…"

"Another time," Vance interrupted. "Teresa, you're my new best friend. I'm Detective Vance Samuelson, and I'm commandeering this phone. I'll get it back to you, okay?'

"Will it really help catch a killer?" Teresa eagerly asked. "Oh, that is soooo going up on my page!"

"Thank you all for your help," I said, as I turned to follow Vance.

"Zack?" Vance asked, several minutes later. "Where'd you land?"

"Remember that first lateral, as Mick called it?"

"Where the river first narrowed and the water sped up?"

I nodded. "Right. I landed in there."

"Ash must be nearby. I'll call it in."

"You know, you didn't have to take that girl's phone," I told my friend.

"We needed a phone, pal. I don't have mine."

I patted my suit and gave Vance a thumbs-up.

"I've got mine." Deciding now was as good a time as any, I decided to start fumbling my way through layers of clothing to retrieve my phone.

"You went in the water," Vance reminded me, without bothering to turn around. He was busy dialing numbers on Teresa's phone. "We need a working phone. I … well, I'll be damned. Had a pre-monition, did you?"

I held up the clear plastic bag in which I had

sealed my phone.

"Not really."

"Then why the bag?" Vance wanted to know. He finished dialing and held the glittery purple phone to his ear.

"Let's just say I didn't want to be the one to ruin it."

Vance turned to look back at me. "Huh?"

"I was afraid I might pee on it, pal."

Vance snorted with laughter. "We weren't supposed to jump, buddy. Why ... Detective Samuelson here. The operation to apprehend Jerod Jones was a bust. We were all drugged. For all I know, the plane ... what's that? It's already landed? Good for them. I'm glad to hear they're all safe. Us? Me and Zack. Yeah, him. We were, uh, forced to deplane at 12,000 feet. Mm-hmm, that's right. Our pal Jerod insisted. Now listen carefully. We still have a chance to apprehend Jerod."

We did? Since when? Curious as hell, I sidled closer to Vance.

"I managed to slip my cell in Jerod's jumpsuit. We already know he's a quick-change artist, so he's bound to discover my phone sooner rather than later. We need to trace my cell phone as soon as possible. Yes, exactly. Yes, I'll hold."

"How the hell did you get your cell phone in his jumpsuit?" I quietly asked.

"Remember the turbulence? When Ash and I both stumbled into Jerod, and we all went down, I managed to tuck my cell into his shirt. Oh, don't look at me like that. He'll figure it out, if he hasn't already done so."

"That's why we need to act now," I guessed. "Nice one, buddy! Where do you think ..."

"I'm here," Vance interrupted. "Yes, sir. It's me, Chief Nelson. No, I'm using a civilian's phone. Mine is hopefully still with the fugitive. The marshal? He was drugged, but still ... uh ... well, he's a persistent guy. He followed the three of us out of the plane. Yes, I can tell you where to find him."

As Vance relayed instructions on where the marshal could be found, and requested an ambulance at the same time, I heard the sounds of an approaching engine. Turning, intent on flagging the motorist down, I raised my arms. But, when the car came into view, I dropped them both with surprise.

I was staring at my Jeep. Jillian was behind the wheel, and both corgis were in the front seat, with their heads visible above the dash. My Jeep skidded to a stop and before I knew it, my fiancée had rushed out of the car and had thrown her arms around me.

"Zachary! What ... oh, my. You're soaking wet! What happened? When I got word that there had been trouble on the plane, I ... I didn't know what to think."

"What are you doing here?" I finally managed to say. I gave Jillian an affectionate hug and then noticed both sets of canine eyes on me. "And the dogs? Let me guess. They knew something was up?"

Jillian nodded. "I'll say. One minute, they're as calm as could be. And the next? Both jumped off the couch and started running in circles, like something had spooked them. Once I let them outside, they ran straight for your Jeep. That's when I knew something bad had happened."

"And you used your phone to track my phone," I guessed. "Nicely done, my dear. Now, could I drive? We need to see if we can nab ourselves one over-confident, pain-in-the-ass mass murderer. Vance! Get over here! We're leaving!"

"Yes, sir," Vance was saying. "I'll keep you posted, sir. Yes, sir. It will be from this number. Or Zack's. Thank you, sir." The detective finished his call and then looked up at Jillian, with surprise etched all over his face. "What the hell? Where did you come from? How did you get here?"

"Two very displeased dogs indicated something was amiss," my fiancée said, as she hurried into the passenger seat. "Sherlock? Watson? Back seat. Keep Vance company."

Both dogs took one look at Vance and practically fought each other to see who'd be first to land in his lap.

"Hi, guys," Vance said, as he gave each dog a thorough scratching. "I don't have anything with me now, but as soon as I do, I'll personally buy each of you a ten pound bag of doggie biscuits."

"Where to?" I asked, as I pulled out of the campground and headed back to town.

While Vance pulled up his phone's location, and wrestled with removing the bright red jumpsuit he was wearing, he read off directions. I filled Jillian in on what had happened as we drove.

"You saved Marshal Binson's life?" Jillian asked, amazed. "I'm so proud of you for keeping your wits about you, Zachary."

"For the record," Vance began, "I didn't know Ash had followed us out of the plane, or I would have ... you know ... not pulled my own cord so quickly."

"Don't sweat it, pal," I assured my friend. "How much farther?'

Vance looked at the purple phone's display. "He's close. Look for somewhere to pull off. It looks like the road widens just around that bend. I think he's there. Stop the car. I had better approach on foot."

While Jillian and I waited in my Jeep, I turned to the corgis and gave each of them a warm welcome. "Hi, guys. No, I'm okay. Don't freak out. Watson? It's not necessary to ... okay, fine. Come here. I'll hold you, just stop wriggling."

My phone started to ring. I took the call on my stereo and was surprised to hear Chief Nelson's voice.

"Hello?"

"Mr. Anderson? Is that you? It's Chief Nelson."

Jillian's eyebrows shot up, as did mine. What was he calling me for?

"Hey there, Chief Nelson. If you're looking for

Vance, he's checking out the area where his phone is supposed to be located. It's just around the bend from us."

"Please tell him Marshal Binson has been located."

"Is he okay?" I worriedly asked.

"He is, yes. His chute became tangled with several trees, and he was suspended nearly twenty feet off the ground, but the paramedics got him down. He's got a few broken ribs, but other than that, he'll be fine. And I hear that's all thanks to you."

"I did what had to be done, sir," I said, shrugging.

"Mm-hmm. I don't know about that. Have Vance call me when he can."

"Will do, sir."

"I'm glad he's okay," Jillian softly said. She took my hand in hers and her eyes teared up. "That was close, Zachary. Too close. I don't want to lose you."

"And you won't," I promised, giving her hand a kiss. "How do I know this? By staying the hell off planes for the foreseeable future."

Vance appeared at the door and hurriedly let himself in.

"Son of a bitch found the phone," Vance grumbled. "I should have known. The little turd even left a note."

"On your phone?" I asked, surprised.

"No, by my phone. It was sitting there, on a

stump. Next to it was a piece of paper and a rock, to hold it down. He knew I would be tracking it. Come on, we need to get back to town. Hey, could I borrow your phone? I need to call Tori as soon as possible."

"Sure, pal," I said, as I handed the phone back to him. "Chief Nelson called. Wants you to call him when you get a chance."

"Yeah, yeah, sure," Vance mumbled, as he hastily dialed a number. "Tor? It's me. Listen, I ... what? You heard about the plane, too? Hey, there's nothing to worry about. Both Zack and I are fine. I don't know about Ash as of yet ..."

"He's going to be fine," I whispered. "He's been found. A few broken ribs, but he'll survive."

Vance nodded his thanks. "What's that? No, there'll be no more trips like that for me. I'll take my mid-life crisis, thank you very much. Listen, don't worry about that right now. I need you to get the girls and get out of the house. Go down to the station, would you? Why? Well, I just want you to be safe."

Alarmed, I shared a look with Jillian. What was going on? In response to my unasked question, Vance handed me a slip of paper. On it were the following words:

Cute. Hope it was worth it.

"From Jerod?" I mouthed.

Vance nodded. I haven't seen him this worried since he had accidentally jabbed himself with a syringe at a crime scene while we were working on a case which involved someone dying by arsenic poisoning.

"They'll be fine," I told Vance, as I stomped on the accelerator. "Jerod's not stupid enough to try for your family, especially not when everyone knows what he looks like."

"He's known for changing his appearance," Vance reminded me. "The smug bastard thinks he can do what he wants, when he wants, and there isn't anyone to stop him. Well, he's not gonna get within ten miles of my family."

"Hear, hear," I added.

We made it back to town in record time. We were headed east on Oregon Street and just made the light at 4th. Turning left, we headed north toward the police station when the unimaginable happened. Both dogs suddenly perked up, walked over Vance's lap, and stared out his window. Sherlock then started firing off warning woofs.

"What are they doing?" Vance wanted to know.

"We're passing the spot where the Square L used to be," I pointed out. "It's part of Gary's Grocery now. Sherlock has barked at this place for quite a while now."

"Grocery store," Vance softly repeated. "No. He's not that stupid, is he? He wouldn't be that bold, would he?"

"What's that?" I asked.

"Zack, stop the car. Go back."

"Go back? To where?"

"The grocery store. I think we need to check it out."

"But ... what about your family?" I protested.

"They're going to the police station," my friend reminded me. "They'll be okay. Hurry, Zack, will you?"

I looked over at Jillian, who shrugged. Turning on the blinker, I flipped a one-eighty and headed back to the grocery store. I parked next to a highway maintenance truck and turned, expectantly, to Vance.

"Now what?"

Vance shrugged. "I'm not sure. I ... wait a minute. I want to check something."

The detective exited my Jeep and inexplicably squatted next to the maintenance truck parked beside us. After a few moments, Vance nonchalantly rose to his feet, reached through my open window and took my phone off the dash, and quickly sent off a few texts.

"What are you doing?" I quietly asked, as though I was now afraid of being overheard.

"I'm investigating a hunch," Vance quietly answered. "Do you see those tires? They're a match for the tracks I found back on that road running parallel to the Rascal."

"It's a maintenance truck," Jillian pointed out. "I'm sure they've probably visited quite a few sections of the surrounding area."

"Probably. I just want to see ... Zack, look down. Jillian? Grab that magazine there and pretend to read it. Whatever you do, don't react to my presence."

Curious as hell, I complied. I watched, mystified, as Vance dropped into a crouch and concealed himself by my front fender. Anxious to see what he was looking at, I turned in my seat to see an older fellow, wearing a dark green jumpsuit with a bright yellow vest over it, slowly approach the truck. He had a large soda in one hand, and a bag of snacks in the other.

It was Jerod's father!

As Jason, or Robert, or whatever his real name was, inserted the key to unlock the driver-side door, Vance suddenly appeared behind him and thrust his gun in Jason's back.

"Hey, pal. Remember me? You look a lot different than the first time I saw you."

Jason finally turned to see Vance standing behind him. The look on his face was priceless.

"You? What the hell ... how did you find ...?"

"That's enough," Vance ordered. A set of handcuffs were produced and quickly snapped into place. "Where's your son? Where's Jerod?"

"You'll never find him," Jason sneered. "He's too smart for the likes of you."

Right on cue, both dogs squirmed in their seats. I think they heard Jason's challenge, and both were saying, in their own way, they accepted it. I quickly unloaded the dogs as the first cop car arrived on the scene. Jason was transferred to the car just as the leashes went taut.

"Jillian, stay put," Vance ordered. "Zack? Lead the way. Find him for me, buddy."

Sherlock and Watson pulled us up to the threshold of the grocery store. I knew dogs were not allowed inside an establishment like that, unless, of course, they were service dogs. Well, I mean, yeah, they were performing a service, but not that type of service. Thankfully, I didn't have to worry about it. Sherlock veered right as we neared the front entry. A few moments later, we were walking along the outside of the store. Then, as if he couldn't make up his mind, we changed direction again. This time, we were heading out across the parking lot. What was that way? Well, if we kept to a straight line, it was one of the Mexican restaurants here, in town: The Lonely Gringo.

My two corgis are fairly well known in town, so the simple act of me walking those two glory-hounds would usually have brought out the townsfolk and their cameras. These two dogs, regardless of where we were, would always end up attracting onlookers. Fortunately for us, no one tried to stop us this time or take their pictures.

We navigated around a large parcel delivery truck that was parked in the outer grocery store parking lot when we saw him. At least, I think it was him. A young man, with his back to us, was casually—but purposefully—headed toward the restaurant. Just like that, the man changed course again and headed west, on Oregon Street.

Both dogs veered left.

"Is that him?" Vance whispered. "Can you tell?"

"He's walking with a purpose," I quietly answered, "and he's changing direction for no reason that I can see. Vance, I think that's him."

I had no sooner finished the sentence when the person we had been following took off like a shot.

"That's him!" Vance cried, overjoyed. "Give me your phone!"

I slapped my phone in Vance's outstretched hand. A split second later, my friend tore off after our fugitive once more. Jillian hurried up to me.

"Was that him?"

I nodded. "Yep. He changed directions a few times, no doubt to see if he was being followed. He must have seen his father being apprehended, so he must have pulled off another quick-change. Lucky for us, Sherlock and Watson were having none of that. They kept leading us straight to him. I hope Vance gets him."

Just then, two of the four cop cars Vance had summoned to the grocery store peeled out of the parking lot and raced west on Oregon Street. Apparently, the other two didn't want to be left out, so they raced off after them, with their sirens so loud it made my ears ring. I waited for the eardrum-splitting noise to fade away, but when it didn't, both Jillian and I turned left to look west. We couldn't see the police cars, but we could hear them. Plus, we could see reflections of their flashing lights. I could only hope that Jerod didn't make it far.

As it turns out, luck had been on Vance's side while in full pursuit of PV's Most Wanted. He told me later that night that Jerod had been about to duck into an open door along Main Street. My guess was Jerod wanted a few private moments so he could try to change his appearance again and slip quietly away. However, as soon as he stepped foot onto Main Street, and started to run for the door, a small, powder-blue car appeared out of nowhere and knocked him flat on his rear. The driver's door had opened and the vehicle owner appeared, spitting mad.

It was Clara Hanson. From what she told the police, it was just a case of mistaken identity. Clara thought Jerod was Marshal Binson and, since she hadn't heard from the marshal, had erroneously assumed he was trying to leave town without paying the bill. Apparently, she had been relentlessly driving through town, looking for him.

Vance rejoined us nearly twenty minutes later. Jillian had ducked into Gary's Grocery to buy herself one of her iced soy latte drinks and a large Coke Zero for me. Vance found us, standing outside my Jeep, entertaining a long line of corgi admirers.

"Vance!" I called, as the detective pushed his way through the small crowd of people. "Tell me you got him."

Vance nodded. "He's been apprehended, but I wasn't the one who got him."

Curiosity piqued, I looked over at Jillian, who

shrugged. "Okay, I'll bite. Who was responsible?"

"Your ardent admirer, Clara," Vance chuckled.

"Clara Hanson caught him?" Jillian incredulously asked. "How is that even possible? She's nothing but a little old lady!"

"She's a little old lady who damn near ran him over with her Prius," Vance clarified. "To be fair, Clara thought Jerod was Ash. She told me she's been looking for him all day. Since she hadn't heard from him, she automatically assumed he was stiffing her."

I covered my ears. "Poor choice of words, buddy."

Vance chuckled and then looked down at the two dogs. He smiled, and without another word, turned on his heel to walk into Gary's Grocery. Five minutes later, he was back, holding two large bags of doggie biscuits. He broke the seal on one bag and offered each corgi a biscuit.

"I'm a man of my word, guys. Here. You earned it. I'll make sure your daddy doesn't try to stiff you for the rest."

J ust remember, you guys said you could make this thing, as strange as it may sound."

"If we have it, then we'll make it," the teenage girl vowed. "What'll you have, Mr. Samuelson?"

"They know you by name?" I asked, amazed. I looked at the girl and hooked a thumb at my friend. "How many times has he been here?"

"Enough that we know what his family likes and dislikes," the girl confided. "Although, this one is new."

Vance enthusiastically rubbed his hands together. "Okay, let's get started. We'll get the normal ones out of the way first. Now, I need a large Hawaiian, thin crust."

The girl tapped away on her ordering screen.

"One medium Canadian bacon, mushroom, and olives," Vance continued, as he grinned at Tori, who nodded her thanks. The detective looked at his two girls and was ready to invite them to order their favorite when Tori suddenly frowned.

"Choose wisely," their mother ordered.

Victoria, the oldest, sighed. Luckily, Tori

turned back to Jillian and continued their conversation. I looked at the young teenager and winked at her.

"What's your favorite?" I whispered.

"Ham and salami," Victoria whispered back.

"And you?" I asked, looking at the younger daughter.

"That works, but add extra ham," Tiffany quietly instructed.

I looked at Victoria, who nodded her approval.

"One medium ham and salami, with extra ham."

Our teenage waitress nodded and entered the order. She looked up, expectantly, to see if there were any more additions. I nodded, as I looked over at Jillian. I knew what her favorite was, and if I played my cards right, I could kill two birds with one stone.

I hastily pulled out the small notebook I had begun to get into a habit of carrying, scribbled down an order, and passed it to Victoria.

"Order that. That should make your mom happy."

Victoria read the note and then grinned. "Umm, okay. I'd like a medium vegetarian, with extra mushrooms, no olives, and no onions. Is this for Ms. Cooper?"

I nodded, knowingly tapped the side of my head, and then reclaimed my notebook.

"We'll take a large combination," another voice announced.

"No, we won't," a female voice contradicted. "We'll have two salad bars, please."

The waitress nodded. "You got it. Will there be anything else?"

Vance nodded. "Just one more. I'd like a small tomato, Tabasco, and peanut butter pizza, please. No cheese. Thank you."

Both of Vance's daughters wrinkled their noses with disgust. I couldn't blame them. That sounded absolutely terrible.

"Where the hell, er, heck did you ever come up with that combination?"

Tiffany held out her hand. Sighing, I handed over a dollar bill for their swear jar.

"It just came to me one night. Thought it might be good, and damned if it wasn't. You should try it."

"Not a chance in hell, pal."

A young hand appeared before me. Rolling my eyes, I handed Vance's youngest daughter another dollar. And who does he think he's fooling? Tabasco, tomatoes, and peanut butter? On a pizza? Gross!

We were (obviously) at a pizza parlor, celebrating Vance's official fortieth birthday. The whole gang was here: Tori and the kids, me and Jillian, and Harry and Julie. Five days had gone by since Jerod's capture. It was all anyone in town could talk about. That, and my heroic act of saving Ash's life. It wasn't that big of a deal. I truly think anyone would have done that, had they been in my position.

We found out the following day that, coming as a surprise to no one, the Daredevils had been disbanded. Thor informed us that he could have kept the club open, only his heart wasn't in it anymore. He couldn't seem to shake the terrible deaths that had occurred, and even though we tried to tell him none of it was his fault, Dean Babcock didn't want to be responsible for anyone's life ever again. That's when Yeti stepped forward and said he'd like to take over the club but start it from scratch. New motto, new outlook, and a new name: The PV Hot Shots. The first thing he did was badger me and Vance relentlessly to join up. Apparently, saving a person's life, while in the middle of a free fall, was held in high esteem with adrenaline clubs.

We were in the midst of going through the list of Yeti's proposed excursions when a familiar face appeared at our table. Looked like our friend, Marshal Binson, had finally been discharged from the hospital. His beard was starting to grow back in, he looked several pounds lighter, and definitely walked with care, but for the most part, he looked good.

"Hey there, amigo!" I exclaimed, as I jumped to my feet. "Pull up a chair and join us. We were just waiting for the pizza to come out."

"I do like this place," Ash admitted, as he slowly pulled a chair from the next table over to ours. "How is everyone doing tonight?"

"I'm officially forty," Vance reported, "and do

you know what? I'm completely fine with it. I have my health, my family, and my career. I don't need anything more than that."

"Good for you," Ash said, and I could tell he meant it.

"Zack," Ash said, as he turned to me, "I haven't had a chance to thank you."

"For …?" I asked.

"For saving my life, obviously. I don't know why you decided to help me out in the middle of a jump, but I'm sure as hell glad you did."

"Any idea when they plan on taking Jerod back to Texas?" Jillian asked.

"They've already left," Ash told us. He checked his watch. "As a matter of fact, they should be there by now."

"Driving?" I asked.

Ash shook his head. "No, sir. They chartered a private jet. They would only fly him, and they weren't about to put him on a commercial airline. The Marshal Service wasn't going to waste any time this time around."

"Didn't you want to do it?" I asked.

"No. I'm no longer a marshal."

"They canned you, bro?" Harry asked. "It wasn't your fault … we were all drugged, man."

"I know that. They know that. However, it's what I wanted. I tendered my resignation as soon as I was able to pick up a phone. I'm just not cut out for the marshal service."

"What will you do?" Tori asked.

"I'm going to return to Virginia," Ash informed us. "That's where my family is. It's best if I find something else to do. With that, I'll take my leave."

Our young waitress appeared at our table, closely followed by two other servers. A series of pizzas were placed in front of us. Our night culminated with the arrival of Vance's god-awful, hot peanut butter goopy pizza. Our entire table fell silent as we stared at the pizza with the red and brown goo on it. Jillian snatched a napkin out of the dispenser and held it over her nose. Figuring it was a good idea, I did the same.

"Good God, man," Ash exclaimed, as he rose from his chair. "What piece of roadkill had to sacrifice its life in order to make that?"

Vance grinned and helped himself to the first slice. "Mmm, this is really good, guys. Would anyone like to try some? Guys?"

When Vance finally looked up from his plate, he was surprised to see everyone had abandoned his table and had joined mine. The smell was so bad we even had to pull our tables apart.

Vance shrugged. "Suit yourself. More for me."

As I sat there and watched one of my friends eat slice after slice of the nastiest-looking pizza I had ever seen, I couldn't help but consider myself lucky. I had a strong circle of friends. I was engaged to a wonderful woman, and I was owner of two adorable dogs who have proven they are still smarter than me. I'd say life was good, but in less than seventy-two hours, I was going to receive a phone call that would shake PV to its core: one of the town's most well-known residents was going to be brutally murdered, and once more, I would be blamed!

AUTHOR'S NOTE

What should have taken only a month or two to write ended up taking four. I shouldn't be making excuses, and I apologize for that, but I did have a few things on my plate that were unexpected. For starters, we moved yet again. I tell you, I am damn tired of moving. However, this was one well worth it. Plus ... this was essentially a double move. We finally moved back into a house, and since it was large enough for all our stuff, we were able to pull all our things out of storage back in Lake Havasu and bring them here.

Yay. More boxes to unload. **sigh**

Many of you will be wondering just what happened to the Dragons of Andela. Well, I'm still working on it. But, seeing how I can release a mystery much faster than an epic fantasy, and especially since the new fantasy is still being developed, my wife suggested I get a couple of CCF titles out of the way. That way, I could focus an extra month or two on completing my new fantasy novel and not be able to release a title for months on end.

With that being said, *Case of the Abandoned Bones* has been started, and will be released this summer! Keep an eye on the blog for all the latest details.

Thanks for reading, everyone! If you enjoyed the novel, please consider leaving a review for it wherever you purchased your copy. It would be greatly appreciated!

J.
June, 2020.

WHAT'S NEXT FOR ZACK AND THE CORGIS?

While working his winery's acreage, Zack is shocked to discover a complete skeleton buried in the ground, undisturbed for decades. Suddenly, the police are taking an interest too, and Zack could be in trouble. The bones of Charles Hanson, father of notorious femme fatale, Clara Hanson, are thought to be linked to a man named Red Dawg, a miner believed to be responsible for the start of the Oregon State Gold Rush in 1850.

Did Charles Hanson discover the hidden location of Red Dawg's gold mine? Could Charlie have been silenced to keep the location a secret? And how can Zack be involved in a Pomme Valley murder that happened 50 years before he showed up! Sherlock and Watson, are on the case as they try, yet again, to keep their buddy Zack out of jail.

Sign up for Jeffrey's newsletter to get all the latest corgi news—
Click here

The Corgi Case Files Series
Available in e-book and paperback

Case of the One-Eyed Tiger
Case of the Fleet-Footed Mummy
Case of the Holiday Hijinks
Case of the Pilfered Pooches
Case of the Muffin Murders
Case of the Chatty Roadrunner
Case of the Highland House Haunting
Case of the Ostentatious Otters
Case of the Dysfunctional Daredevils
Case of the Abandoned Bones

Case of the Great Cranberry Caper

If you enjoy Epic Fantasy, check out Jeff's other series:
Pirates of Perz
Tales of Lentari
Bakkian Chronicles

Manufactured by Amazon.ca
Bolton, ON